Geronimo Stilton

Thea Stilton
THE SECRET OF THE SNOW

Scholastic Inc.

Library of Congress Cataloging-in-Publication Data Available

ISBN 978-0-545-65605-4

Based on an original idea by Elisabetta Dami.
www.geronimostilton.com

Published by Scholastic Inc., 557 Broadway, New York, NY 10012.

Text by Thea Stilton
Original title *Il segreto delle Fate delle Nevi*
Cover by Flavio Ferron
Illustrations by Giuseppe Facciotto, Danilo Barozzi, Chiara Balleello, and Barbara Pellizzari (design), and Alessandro Muscillo (color)
Graphics by Marta Lorini

Special thanks to Tracey West
Translated by Julia Heim
Interior design by Kay Petronio

14 13 12 11 10 18 19 20 21 22/0

Printed in China 38

First printing, September 2014

THEA STILTON AND THE THEA SISTERS

THE LAND OF MINWA

The Land of Minwa is a fantasy land where magical creatures live. They are based on creatures from Japanese myths and Japanese folktales known as *mukashi banashi*. Some of their names and abilities, however, are unique to this strange world.

TANUKI: This mischievous creature can shape-shift into almost anything. In Japan, its true form is thought to be a raccoon-dog, a type of wild canine.

TENGU: These mysterious, birdlike creatures have red wings. They live in the Forest of the Dancing Pines and are expert potion makers.

OROCHI: This dragon has eight tails and eight heads, and each head has an angry temper. If Orochi is guarding a bridge, you must ask permission before crossing.

THE SNOW FAIRIES: They live along the banks of the Frosty River. Their breath can turn things into ice.

KITSUNE: These beautiful fairies have long, foxlike tails. Each one carries a mysterious golden sphere.

KAPPA: These peaceful water creatures have delicate skin and resemble turtles. They know all about natural healing remedies.

KIJIMUNA: Experts at fishing and navigation, these fairylike creatures are very unfriendly. It's best not to ride in their boats unless you have to.

UMIBOZU: This enormouse creature resembles an octopus. Legend says that it tips over boats that come close to it . . . but it may not be as mean as it looks.

BAKU: These creatures can visit the dreams of those who live in the Land of Minwa. In this world, the baku looks like a tiny, colorful elephant.

LAUGHING FAIRIES: They are full of information about the Land of Minwa — but they can't stop laughing long enough to share it.

MERRY CHRISTMAS!

"A little bit higher," Colette instructed Paulina, who was placing a sparkly **glass star** on the big spruce tree at the entrance to **MOUSEFORD ACADEMY.**

"Stop! Hang it right next to that **SILVER** ball."

Paulina smiled down at her. "It's perfect, Colette. You have such an eye for these things."

The festive atmosphere of **CHRISTMAS** filled the air at the academy. The semester was over, and students were **happy** and excited for the holidays. They all pitched in, stringing **colored lights** and decorations through the halls.

The Thea Sisters had offered to decorate

It's beautiful!

the huge tree that stood at the academy entrance. Each year, it was decorated in a different theme.

This year's theme was SNOW, and the five friends thought it was perfect. The magical silver and **SPARKLING** white colors were enchanting, and reminded them of the **fantastic** adventures they'd had together.

"I made an ornament for the tree," **Violet** said shyly. She carefully opened a small box that she held in her paws.

"**Cheese niblets!** It's beautiful!" Pamela exclaimed. "Did you really make this yourself?"

Violet nodded and held up the ornament — a BLUE GLASS ball with a perfect replica of Mouseford Academy nestled in the snow inside it.

Nicky looked stunned. "Where did you learn to make things like that?"

"My grandfather taught me when I was young," Violet explained. "He would spend hours making MODELS of ships to put inside bottles. So I thought to myself, why not try it with a glass ball, and our school?"

"It's fabumouse, Vi!" Colette exclaimed. "It makes the tree even more beautiful."

"Gee, snow. Could this year's theme be even more boring?" a familiar voice asked.

The friends turned to see Ruby Flashyfur behind them. She loved to make trouble for the Thea Sisters.

"Hi, Ruby," Nicky said with a friendly smile. "Would you like to help us decorate the tree? We really have some beautiful ornaments for it."

Ruby shrugged. "Sorry, but I have

something much better to do."

She paused, waiting for someone to ask her what it was. But the **THEA SISTERS** weren't interested. They turned back to the decorations.

"Well," Ruby continued, sounding annoyed, "I am getting ready to leave for the holidays. I'm going to an exclusive ski resort in the mountains."

"Okay, well, have fun," Colette replied casually.

Ruby clenched her **paws**, turned around, and walked away with her snout in the air. The Thea Sisters **LOOKED** at one another — they knew Ruby well, and this was just like her. Then they continued decorating the tree.

A SURPRISE INVITATION

While the Thea Sisters were busy decorating the great Christmas tree, I was busy planning my next class on **adventure journalism** that I would teach at Mouseford Academy.

I am friends with Octavius de Mousus, the academy's headmaster, and he had invited me to come to the school for the holiday **festivities**. In my free time, I could work on a curriculum for the class.

There was *so much* I wanted to cover! The desk in my office was covered with papers, notes, and lessons plans. Then, from somewhere under that mountain of paper, came the sound of my cell phone **ringing**.

I dug under the papers and answered it.

"Good morning, Thea." I heard. "It's **Will Mystery** from the Seven Roses Unit."

"Will! It's so great to hear from you. What's new?" I asked.

Will works at the **INSTITUTE OF INCREDIBLE STORIES** (I.I.S.), the top secret organization that deals with unsolved mysteries. He is the head of the **SEVEN ROSES UNIT**, the most mysterious

Hello, Thea!

department of the I.I.S.

"Did you get my letter?" he asked me.

"I haven't opened my **MAIL** yet," I replied. "Hold on."

I put down the phone and looked through the **heap** of envelopes on my desk. I saw it and ***quickly*** opened it.

Dear Thea,

The Thea Sisters have proven themselves to be an important asset for our research into fantasy worlds. Do you think they would be able to come to the I.I.S. as soon as they have some time off from school? We would like them to attend a course in the langua-ges of mythic lands. When they arrive, they will find many surprises waiting for them!

Thanks for your help,

Will Mystery

I.I.S.
The Institute of Incredible Stories

MYSTERIES . . . BENEATH THE ICE!

The I.I.S., the Institute of Incredible Stories, is a research center dealing with unsolved mysteries. Its headquarters are in a hidden location under the glaciers of Antarctica.

MYTHS AND LEGENDS

The Seven Roses Unit is the most secret department of the I.I.S. This branch studies fantasy worlds, which are inhabited by characters from myths and legends.

Special Maps

In the Hall of the Seven Roses, there are living maps of all of the fantasy worlds. They change when any land changes and show when a land is in danger.

The Power of Music

A special glass elevator travels between the I.I.S. and the fantasy worlds. Only Will Mystery can make it work, using special music.

I picked up the phone. "Will? I just read it. The THEA SISTERS will be thrilled!"

"Excellent," said Will. "They have helped the I.I.S. solve two challenging mysteries already. Do you think they will agree to come this time as well?"

"I think so," I said. "Their holiday break is just beginning, so they don't have any classes. I will RUSH right off and tell them!"

Will told me the rest of the details as I RACED through the halls to find the five friends. I couldn't wait to give them the wonderful news!

THE BEST PRESENT EVER

When I reached the Thea Sisters, they were **happily** exchanging gifts in the room they shared.

"Thea! We have a present for you," Nicky said. "Come on in."

"I have a gift for all of you as well," I said.

"That is so nice of you, Thea," said Paulina.

"It's a gift that you can't see, but I know you'll like it a lot," I said with a **mysterious** smile.

The friends gathered around me, **curious**. "I just spoke to Will Mystery," I explained. "He has invited you all back to the I.I.S.!"

"*What is this about, Thea?*" asked Colette.

"He wants you to take a course in the

Am I interrupting?
Thea! Come in!

languages of **FANTASY** lands," I said.

"That is **MOUSETASTIC** news!" Pam cheered.

"When do we leave?" Nicky asked.

"You can leave today, if you'd like," I replied. "I just need to confirm with Will."

"**We'd love to!**" they all said at once.

I grinned. "Perfect. Will said he could have someone here for you in two hours."

Paulina clapped her paws together. "What a wonderful **surprise** this is! Just imagine! We will learn how to communicate with creatures from other worlds."

How wonderful!

"I wish I could go, too, but I'm busy here," I said. "But I'll be with you in **spirit**. Now, get those bags packed!"

"How long will we be away?" Colette asked. "I need to make sure I don't repeat any outfits."

"And I need to make sure I pack enough cheese crackers," added Pam.

"You'll return in one week," I replied.

Nicky picked up a PRESENT wrapped in RED PAPER and tied with a shiny gold ribbon. "Then you have to open the gift we got you right now!"

"You shouldn't have!" I exclaimed, and I was really touched. It was sweet of my students to remember me during the holidays.

I untied the ribbon, unwrapped the paper, and found a beautiful LILAC sweater inside.

"It's marvemouse!" I exclaimed, hugging them one by one.

"Try it on! Then we can see if Colette guessed the right size," Nicky urged.

"Of course I got it right," Colette said. "I know fashion."

I put on the sweater; it was really soft and perfectly WARM. "I love it! Thank you!" I said.

Paulina nodded. "It looks really good on you."

"I will call Will Mystery and tell him you're coming," I informed them. "Then I'll meet you at the heliport in two hours to say good-bye."

I left the room, and the sweater felt like a nice warm HUG.

I'M SO LUCKY TO HAVE STUDENTS LIKE THOSE MOUSELETS!

DESTINATION: I.I.S.

Will Mystery had told me that he would send an I.I.S. **agent** for the girls. The agent would take them by **helicopter** out to the open sea. There, they would connect with Will, who would be waiting for them on a **SUBMARINE**. Then he would take them to the secret location of the I.I.S.

It might sound like a lot of steps, but it was necessary to keep the location of the I.I.S. and the Seven Roses Unit a **SECRET**. If word that fantasy worlds really existed fell into the wrong paws, it could be disastrous.

The Thea Sisters arrived at the heliport packed and ready.

"Do you have your PENDANTS?" I asked them.

In reply, they all showed me the rose-shaped CRYSTAL pendants that Will had given them. Each pendant was like a personal I.D. card. It contained information about each mouse and allowed her access into the SEVEN ROSES UNIT.

"Keep in touch over the week," I requested. "I'd love to hear how things are going."

"Of course we will!" PAULINA assured me.

The Thea Sisters said good-bye and boarded the helicopter. It took off with a rumble and flew into the blue sky above Whale Island.

I waited until the helicopter disappeared from view before I went back to my office. I was EXCITED for the five friends! I knew they would all do well in the course, and would probably have a lot of FUN, too.

I had no idea that they were in for much more than a class — they were headed for another **adventure**! It began when, after flying across the ocean for an hour, the helicopter descended toward a **platform** on what looked like a large oil rig.

"Aren't we meeting Will on the submarine?" Colette asked the I.I.S. agent piloting the helicopter.

He SHRUGGED. "All I know is that I'm supposed to bring you here."

The friends exchanged confused glances.

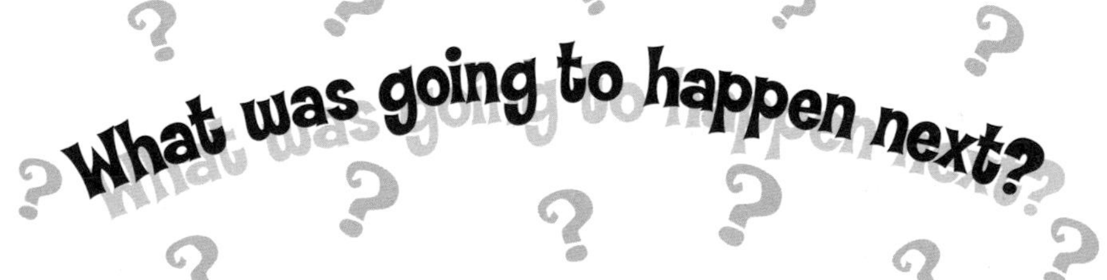

EMERGENCY ARRIVAL

The Thea Sisters got out of the helicopter.

"I don't see Will anywhere," Paulina said, looking around.

"There's a door down there," Colette said, pointing to a *building* on the rig's platform.

Pam started jogging toward it. "Let's check it out!"

The others followed her as the helicopter **TOOK OFF** behind them. They opened the door and found themselves inside a HALLWAY with a map of the building on the wall.

Paulina pointed to the **map**. "Look, there's the control room. Let's head there. Maybe we'll find someone in charge."

Let's go!

They followed the map and made their way through the mazelike halls, swiftly reaching the control room.

"May we come in?" Paulina asked, pushing open the door.

But the room was empty, except for rows of computers, monitors, and SWITCHES on the wall.

Paulina eagerly looked around. "This is amazing. From here we can control all of the rig's equipment, and check on the quarters of the crew."

"WHAT CREW?" Nicky complained. "There's nobody here!"

"Most important, Will Mystery isn't here," Colette pointed out. "I really don't understand why that helicopter abandoned us in the middle of the ocean."

"It is very strange," Pam agreed. "Last

time, Will met us on the submarine."

Suddenly a **metallic** voice came over the ship's **SPEAKERS**.

"Welcome, Thea Sisters! My name is NR961 and I am the latest in computer technology," the voice said. "In the refrigerator there are cold drinks for you."

At those words, a door in the wall opened to reveal a refrigerator full of bottled water, **FRUIT JUICES**, and salty and sweet snacks.

"Look! **Cheese sticks!**" Pam said happily.

"The snacks look great, but I still don't understand why Will isn't here," Colette said.

"Maybe he is in charge of an IMPORTANT investigation, and can't get away," Paulina suggested.

"Well, he could have texted us," Colette pointed out.

Then NR961 began speaking again.

"In the room on your left you will find oxygen tanks, thermal suits, and a portal with access to the sea. Your **mission** is to reach the Seven Roses Unit by swimming there. End of transmission."

The Thea Sisters looked at one another, **perplexed**.

Violet spoke up. "NR961, are you there?"

The computer didn't answer. Then the **lights** on the monitors turned off. A *worried* silence hung in the air.

Cheese sticks!

"Well, we don't have much choice," Nicky concluded. "Let's see what this is about."

They headed into the next room, and found wet suits and **oxygen tanks** waiting for them, just as NR961 had said. It was everything they would need for *deep-sea swimming*.

"But how will we **KNOW** where to swim?" Violet asked.

Paulina picked up a piece of paper and a **COMPASS**. "Here's a note that says to swim northeast. We can use the compass to guide us."

"Sounds like a plan," said Nicky. The Thea Sisters donned their **SCUBA GEAR** and exited the building.

Then they dove into the deep blue sea.

THE ENTRANCE IN THE ROCK

The Thea Sisters swam underwater, past strange-looking plants and **COLORFUL** fish. They followed Paulina, who held the compass in her paw.

Soon they came to a **ROCKY** wall. Paulina suddenly had a terrible feeling. The last time they had been to the I.I.S., Will used a remote to open a **DOOR** in the wall. How would they get in now?

Then Nicky started waving her paw, motioning for the others to follow her. They swam around a corner and saw ***BRIGHT LIGHT*** pouring from a hole in the wall.

THEY HAD FOUND THE ENTRANCE!

Excited, the Thea Sisters swam through the **crack** in the rock. They followed the **bright light** to a landing. As they emerged above the water, they saw Will Mystery looking down at them!

"**Welcome!**" he called out. He helped them as one by one they climbed the ladder to the landing. Once they were out of their scuba gear, he grinned at them.

"Excellent!" he said. "I knew that all of you would **pass the test** with no trouble."

"Test? What are you talking about?" Nicky asked.

"Your underwater trip from the oil rig to the entrance of the **SEVEN ROSES UNIT** was an exercise," Will replied. "We put all of our agents through it."

"**Cheese niblets!**" Pam exclaimed. "We had no idea what was going on."

"It felt like you forgot about us," Colette said.

"Yet you didn't give up or **PANIC**," Will pointed out. "That is precisely the point of the test. We need rodents with **SPECIAL GIFTS** to work in this department, and you just proved that you have them."

"What kind of gifts?" Colette asked.

"You need the ability to work as a **UNITED TEAM**," Will replied.

Nicky nodded. "We are a good team," she said.

"And that's not all," Will said. "You also have good intuition, you solve problems quickly, and you remain calm in tough situations. Those are all qualities we need at the INSTITUTE OF INCREDIBLE STORIES."

The Thea Sisters exchanged happy glances.

WILL WAS RIGHT!
THE FIVE OF THEM WERE A REAL TEAM. THEY WERE READY TO FACE ANY CHALLENGE!

A STRANGE GUEST

Will Mystery led the Thea Sisters to the HALL OF THE SEVEN ROSES, the center of the department. They sat down at a big, round table. In front of each of them was a laptop.

"We'll start with an introduction to the course in **fantasy languages**," Will began. "Then you can get settled in your quarters. I'm sure —"

Suddenly, mysterious MUSIC began to flow from the glass elevator in the middle of the hall. The friends gasped. They knew that the ELEVATOR was a way to travel between the Seven Roses Unit and the fantasy worlds. Who could be on it?

The doors to the elevator BURST open,

revealing a passenger inside.

"It's a . . . teapot?" Violet asked.

The girls stared at it for a moment, puzzled, and then the teapot JUMPED up! It spun around wildly.

"I think I understand," Will said, slowly stepping toward the elevator.

"Careful, Will!" Paulina cried out.

Will took another step closer, and the teapot hopped back. Will reached out to grab him, but the teapot spun around quickly, escaping him. Will paused . . . and then reached out suddenly, catching the teapot by surprise.

"Got it!" Will exclaimed.

"How can a teapot move like that?" Violet wondered.

Will didn't answer. They watched, curious, as he placed the teapot on the table. Then, to

A teapot?

their surprise, he began to **tickle** it!

The big teapot responded by jumping into Will's arms. Very slowly, it began to **CHANGE** shape, right in front of their eyes!

"Look! A *tail*!" Paulina exclaimed.

"And those are **PAWS**!" added Colette.

Pam's eyes were wide. "Cheesecake! Now the thing's got **ears**!"

As they watched, the creature took on a completely new form.

"It's a **raccoon**!" Nicky cried.

"He looks like a raccoon, but he's not," said Will. "He is actually a magical creature called a **TANUKI**. They are jokesters, and love to play tricks. Tanuki can *shapeshift* into almost any object or creature. To make them turn back to their true form, you have to tickle them."

"So he turned into a teapot just to be

funny?" Violet asked. She couldn't take her eyes off the **furry** little creature with the bushy tail.

"He might just be joking," Will mused, "or maybe he has a **message** for us."

"**WHERE** does he come from?" asked Colette.

"From the **LAND OF MINWA**," Will replied. "The creatures there are related to **JAPANESE** mythology and traditional

folktales known as *mukashi banashi.*"

"Japanese tales are fascinating," said Violet.

Will nodded. "Many interesting creatures live in the Land of Minwa," he said. "Some are basically harmless, like this tanuki. But others are quite DANGEROUS."

Colette shuddered. "You mean, like MONSTERS?"

"Yes, we believe there are some monsters there," Will answered. "But if you remember from your adventures in the Land of Erin, even beautiful creatures can be dangerous."

"So how can we be sure that this cute little guy is okay?" Pam asked, nodding to the raccoon.

"According to the tales, tanuki are MISCHIEVOUS but usually good-hearted," said Will.

"Ahem," coughed the tanuki. "Excuse

me, but may I please say something?"

The tanuki knew how to talk!

The Thea Sisters looked stunned. Only Will didn't look surprised.

"Why are you here?" he asked the raccoon.

"I got **LOST**!" the tanuki responded.

Now Will *did* look surprised. The glass elevator was difficult to locate unless you were looking for it. Could the tanuki really have just **stumbled** on it?

"So where am I?" the little creature asked.

"I'm sorry, but I can't tell you — this is a **SECRET** location," Will responded firmly. "But maybe we can help you if you tell us what happened."

The tanuki **FROWNED** at him. "How do I know I can trust you?"

"We are here to help creatures from fantasy

lands," Will replied.

"My name is Will Mystery," he went on. "And this is PAULINA, **Violet**, *Colette*, PAMELA, and *Nicky*."

"**Don't be afraid**," said Violet sweetly. "We just want to help."

The tanuki relaxed. "I was running quickly, to escape a **snowstorm**," he began. "I needed shelter, and I found that . . . thingy." He nodded behind him to the glass elevator.

"Then I arrived here," he continued. "And maybe it's a good thing that I did. **Strange things** have been happening where I live."

"What kind of strange things?" Will asked.

The tanuki's expression grew serious. "The precious **LOTUS FLOWERS** that grow in the Land of Minwa are disappearing. It is a terrible thing for all of us who live there!"

DANGER IN THE LAND OF MINWA!

Will Mystery walked toward the Living Map on the floor of the Hall of the Seven Roses.

"He is right!" Will exclaimed. "See? There are two SHADOWS over the Land of Minwa. That means that there is a danger threatening the land. But there may be time to fix it.

THEA SISTERS, A NEW MISSION AWAITS US!"

"We're with you!" Paulina replied quickly.

"We must go to the Land of Minwa with the tanuki, and find out why the LOTUS FLOWERS are disappearing," Will said.

"Shouldn't we tell Thea about this?" Violet asked.

Will started typing into his phone. "I will

Look!

send Thea a coded message," he said. "Maybe she can join us."

Then he nodded to the Thea Sisters.

"Now come with me!" he told them. "There is something we must do before we leave."

He picked up the tanuki in his arms and led the Thea Sisters out of the Hall of Roses and into a long hallway. They followed him, CURIOUS.

Will stopped in front of a closed door. He took out his rose-shaped pendant and slipped it into an opening carved into the wall. The door opened into a dark room.

Will turned on the light, and the Thea Sisters gasped when they saw what was inside.

AN ACCELERATED COURSE

"Welcome to our accelerated learning room!" Will said proudly.

The room looked like a scene from a science fiction movie. Arranged in a circle were strange-looking **pods** with thick cords attached to them. Above each pod was a computer monitor.

"What are those for?" Paulina asked.

"A student lies in the pod and puts on the **HEADPHONES**," Will explained. "A full course of study is then transmitted into the student's brain."

"So, we'll learn everything about the Land of Minwa **INSTANTLY**?" Pam asked.

"Not exactly," Will explained. "Your brain

What do you think?
Wow!

will hold the information. But you won't be able to retrieve it unless you need it."

Pam sighed. "It seemed **too good** to be true."

"But it is all we have time for now," Will said. "Long-term studying is the best way to retain information, but we developed our ***accelerated*** learning machine to deal with emergencies like this. I'll show you how it works if one of you will volunteer."

"*I'll do it!*" Paulina offered eagerly.

The tanuki was **DOZING** in Will's arms, and Will gently set him down. He instructed Paulina to lie down in the pod and then placed the headphones over her ears.

"Next, I will lower the cover of the pod," Will explained. "You will close your eyes, and I will **ACTIVATE** the commands to begin the procedure. You'll hear a few beeps, and then you'll see flashes of light, even though your eyes are closed."

Paulina nodded. "Okay. I'm ready!"

Will closed the pod, and then quickly started typing on a control panel. Letters, numbers, and IMAGES popped up on the monitor above the pod, scrolling with such SPEED that they began to blur together.

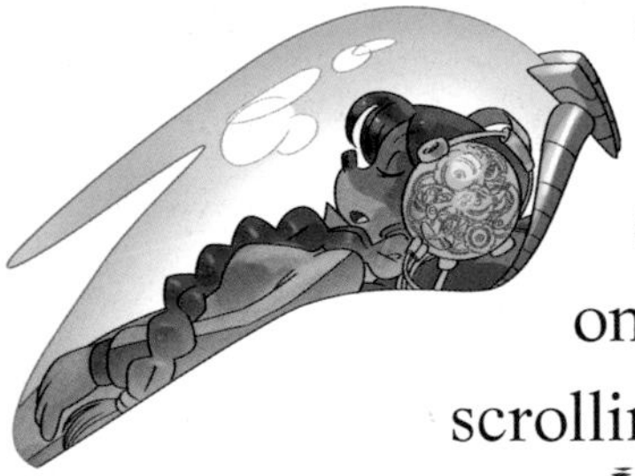

After a few minutes, the monitor went blank. The cover of the pod lifted open. The Thea Sisters watched, holding their breath until Paulina opened her EYES.

"That was fabumouse!" Paulina exclaimed, taking off her headphones.

"What do you remember?" Colette asked.

"I'm . . . I'm not sure," Paulina said.

"It doesn't work that way," Will explained.

"The information will return to your mind only if something **triggers** it."

Nicky shook her head. "Unbelievable!"

"Now the rest of you can take the course," Will said. *Nicky*, PAM, **Violet**, and *Colette* each climbed into a **pod**, and Paulina and Will helped them put on their headphones. When the four pods were closed, Will typed into the **control panel** and then turned to Paulina.

"We're good to go," he said. "I'm going to pack some EQUIPMENT for our trip. You're in charge until I get back."

"I'll keep an eye on them," Paulina promised. She felt **PROUD** knowing that Will trusted her.

When he returned, the four mice were out of their pods.

"I can tell the information is in my **BRAIN**

somewhere," Nicky said. "It's **AMAZING**."

"Except those headphones flattened my fur!" Colette complained. Everyone laughed.

"Good. Now we just have to wait for THEA," Will said.

"And wake up our friend," Nicky added, glancing at the sleeping TANUKI.

"He **HIBERNATES** this time of year. The emergency must have woken him," Will guessed. Then he carefully picked up the raccoon, and they all returned to the HALL OF THE SEVEN ROSES.

CODED MESSAGES

While the Thea Sisters took their accelerated learning course, I was finishing up work in my office at **MOUSEFORD ACADEMY**.

"Last one!" I said, filing some **papers** into a folder with satisfaction. All I had to do now was prepare my presentation for the teachers' meeting.

Then a sudden sound made me **JUMP**. It was an alarm, coming from my laptop. I knew what that noise meant:

I had a coded message from Will Mystery!

I copied the text and pasted it into my **decoding** program. Then I read the secret message.

Dear Thea:

Meet us at the I.I.S. as soon as you can! The Land of Minwa is in danger! We need to leave immediately. We will wait for you at the glass elevator.

Thanks,
Will

P.S. Please bring some heavy sweaters for the Thea Sisters. It's pretty cold down there.

There was no time to lose. I erased the message and turned off my computer. Then I raced to my room, changed into WARM winter clothes, and grabbed a big bag.

I went to the Thea Sisters' room and found everything I needed in their closets. Then, on a hunch, I headed for the dock.

There I found the **Rose of the Seas** motorboat waiting for me, like I always do when I leave for an I.I.S. mission. An **agent** nodded hello at me as I boarded, and then we took off without a word.

After a short trip, the agent stopped the boat in the middle of the sea. Soon, the periscope of the I.I.S. SUBMARINE poked above the water.

Minutes later I was on the sub, *speeding* toward the I.I.S.'s secret headquarters. As soon as I arrived I headed right for the Hall of the Seven Roses. Will's mysterious message hadn't told me much, and I was anxious to learn what was happening in the **LAND OF MINWA**.

As soon as I stepped into the hall, Will and the Thea Sisters rushed over to me, talking excitedly all at once. What a **warm** welcome!

"*Glad you made it!*" Will said, shaking my paw.

"With your help, we can do this!" said Colette.

"I'm confused," I told them. "Can you explain what's going on? First, though, here are the clothes that Will asked for."

I gave them the heavy bag of clothing. Then I noticed a raccoon sleeping in a chair. "Who is this little guy?" I asked.

"It's a tanuki, a shape-changing creature," Will replied. "He's from the Land of Minwa."

"He said there is a great **DANGER** threatening his world," Nicky added.

"The LOTUS FLOWERS that grow there are disappearing, and no one knows why," said Violet, worried.

"The flowers are **PRECIOUS** to the inhabitants of the Land of Minwa," Paulina concluded. "We need to find out why they are VANISHING."

I nodded. "Then there is no time to lose. Let's go!"

Will turned to the Thea Sisters. "Are you ready?"

"**READY!**" they replied in unison.

Will woke the tanuki, and we all went to the glass elevator, the secret portal between the fantasy worlds.

"Why don't you open the door, Colette?" Will asked.

Colette stepped forward, took the pendant from around her neck, and said her name.

The door opened and we all entered the elevator.

Will punched in the destination on the control panel and **sweet music** began to play all around us.

"What instrument is this?" Violet wondered. "It sounds almost like a guitar."

"It's called a **shamisen**. It's a Japanese **THREE-STRINGED** instrument," Colette replied, and then gasped. "It works! The information just popped into my head, like you said it would, Will."

"Unfortunately, you'll only be able to remember little bits of **information** at a time," Will said. "But as you can see, it comes in handy."

Then a chorus of voices joined the music. It sang the same words over and over without stopping.

"Land of Minwa... Land of Minwa... Land of Minwa... Land of Minwa... Land of Minwa... Land of Minwa... Land of Minwa... Land of Minwa..."

Then the doors of the elevator opened, revealing a bright white landscape that made everyone squint.

We had arrived in the Land of Minwa!

How exciting!

It's fantastic!
There's so much snow!

THE LAND OF MINWA

When our eyes got used to the light, we stared openmouthed at the **BEAUTY** of the scene in front of us. It was like we had been absorbed into a book of Japanese folktales. **Snow-capped** mountains rose in the distance, and in the valley below were villages of tiny houses. Their pointy roofs looked like they had been **SPRINKLED** with Parmesan cheese.

"Hey, where did the tanuki go?" Nicky asked, breaking the silence.

We spun around. He wasn't in the **elevator**, and we couldn't see him anywhere around us. Then I noticed something in the **snow**.

"**Footprints**," I said, pointing.

Nicky looked at them carefully.

"See how the prints of the two back feet

are side by side? They could be RABBIT prints, not raccoon prints," she said.

"But the tanuki couldn't have vanished into thin air," Pam said, frustrated.

"Things aren't always as they seem in these fantasy worlds, Pam," Will pointed out. "Remember, the tanuki is a shape-shifting prankster, and now he is back in his own world."

"So should we be looking for a *teapot*?" Violet asked, **remembering** how the tanuki had first appeared to them.

Paulina's eyes lit up. "Or maybe a rabbit!" she cried, pointing to the footprints.

"Good thinking!" Will said.

So, we followed the **footprints** through the snow,

Look at those footprints!

searching for the tanuki as a rabbit. As untrustworthy as he was, that little animal was our only **guide** in that unknown and dazzling world.

Pam looked around the vast, snowy landscape. "It's too bad we don't have a map," she said. "Then maybe we'd have a better idea of where we're going."

"Yes, a map would be useful in this mysterious place," Will agreed. "All we can do is keep our eyes wide open."

The rabbit's tracks led us to a forest with trees that looked like giant sticks of cotton candy. Snow crystals that sparkled in the sun covered all of the tree branches.

"The TANUKI headed in there," Will said, pointing to the footprints. "Come on, LET'S GO into the forest!"

Let's go!

THE TANUKI'S RIDDLES

"I see a rabbit!" Paulina exclaimed, pointing to the furry creature perched on a **snow-covered** rock ahead of us on the path. But it didn't look like an ordinary rabbit.

"It's **fuchsia**!" Nicky cried.

"How fashionable!" Colette commented.

We all laughed, and Colette **CAUTIOUSLY** approached the animal.

"**TANUKI**, is that you?" she asked. We still weren't sure.

"Or am I a frog?" the rabbit responded, and it burst out laughing. Then its **fur**

started to vanish and its skin turned green. It turned into a BIG FROG right in front of our eyes!

"What is going on?" Pam said.

The tanuki got quiet, and we hoped that it wasn't offended.

"We appreciate your fun-loving spirit, but we need to figure out the mystery of the LOTUS FLOWERS," I said diplomatically. "Can you help us?"

"Oh, all right!" the tanuki said with a HUFF.

His skin started to change from green to brown . . . then fur sprouted all over his body. Two POINTY EARS popped up, and then the tanuki was a raccoon again!

"Good work, Thea!" Colette whispered.

Will didn't waste any time. "Can you tell us where we are?" he asked the raccoon.

"We are in the SAKURA FOREST," the tanuki replied.

"*Sakura* means 'CHERRY BLOSSOM' in Japanese," Will told us.

"Very good!" said the tanuki, his eyes twinkling. "Now, here is a **prize** for you."

He clapped his front paws together and three **red cherries** appeared in Will's paw. Curious, Violet walked to the nearest tree and shook one of the branches. The snow sprinkled off, revealing light pink flowers growing on the branch.

"How can the tree bloom in winter?" she wondered.

"Our magical cherry trees BLOOM all year long," replied the tanuki. "They are a constant breath of springtime, and they bring us much joy."

He sighed. "They are a great comfort, especially now during these **sad** times."

"If you are sad about the lotus flowers, then help us figure out what is happening to them," Colette said.

The tanuki frowned. "That is very **difficult**, because everyone is blaming everyone else!"

Will nodded. "I understand. Do you at least know where we can find a **map** of this land? That would be a big help."

"There are no maps of the Land of Minwa," the raccoon replied, shaking his head.

"Well, I could try to **draw** one as we go," Paulina offered.

Will nodded. "That would be a very useful thing to have in our files," he said, handing her a pen and paper.

The tanuki produced a **blue pen** out of nowhere. “Use this!”

“I’ve got one already,” Paulina said, starting to draw with Will’s pen. But it didn’t work!

The tanuki waved the PEN under her snout. “Try this one! It writes for sure.”

Paulina took the pen from the raccoon’s paws. It worked just fine. “Thanks!” she said.

The tanuki responded with a **mysterious** smile.

“Can you at least tell us where we should start looking?” Pam asked him.

He shrugged. “*North? South? Here? There?* That’s up to you.”

Pam looked at her friends, frustrated. The tanuki wasn’t being very helpful. Then he suddenly began speaking in rhyme.

“If a beginning is what suits you,
then I have ready a nice little clue!”

He began to **blow** on the cherry trees. The **PINK PETALS** of the cherry blossoms began to fall onto the **snow**.

We watched, enchanted, as the petals formed words in front of our eyes.

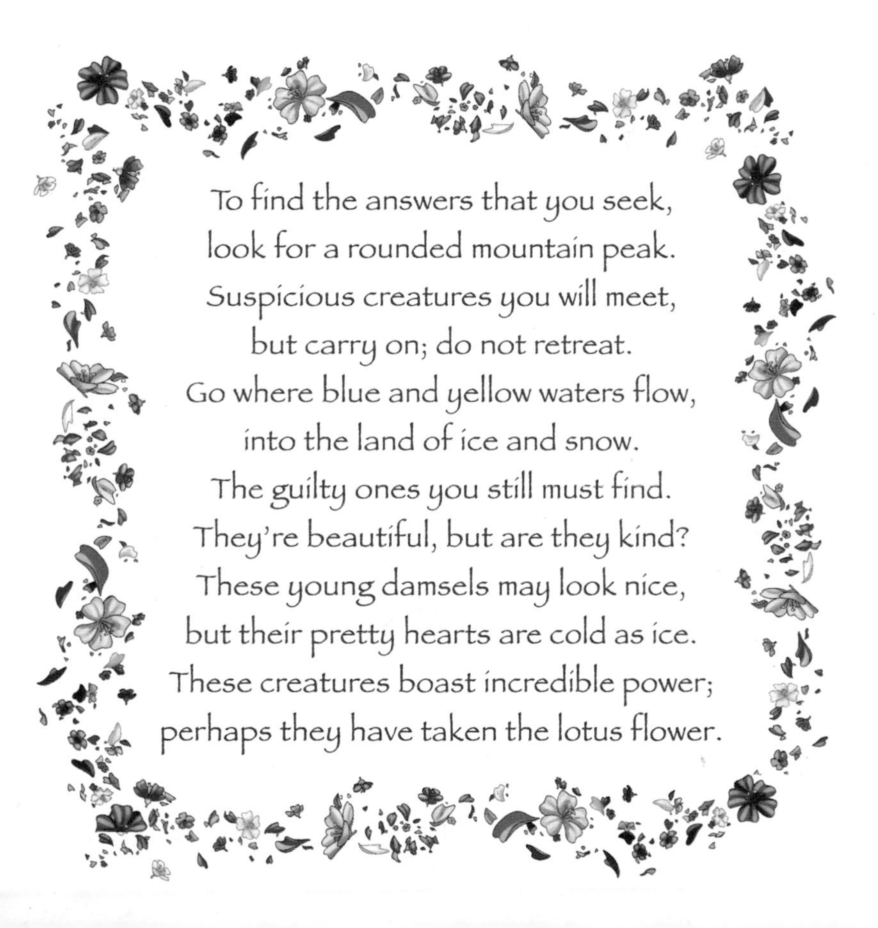

"It's a riddle!" Nicky exclaimed.

"What does it mean?" Pam asked.

"Wait, there's another one!" Paulina cried, as a new **SHOWER OF PETALS** began to fall. They formed new words on top of the snow.

In abysses is where he hides:
it's the great and evil Lord of Tides.
Sovereign of all, he rules the land.
Oh, terrible things does he demand!
Nay, he simply cannot stand
anything that grows on land.
Do start your journey to the sea.
Exactly three fins are what you will see.

As we stared at the petals in disbelief, the tanuki began to scamper away.

"Each of the riddles is **DIFFERENT**,"

Paulina said thoughtfully. "One says to look for mountains, and the other says we're supposed to go to the sea. Which one is right?"

The tanuki stopped and looked back at Paulina.

"Of paths to follow, there are two
that will reveal the mystery to you.
One is salty, one is sweet,
but neither path leads to defeat.
Don't ask me which way to tread.
Just open your eyes and look ahead!"

Then he **RAN OFF** into the white snow.

We all looked at one another, confused.

"Well, that was STRANGE!" Nicky remarked.

THE SOLUTION!

The tanuki had put us to the test with his riddles, but we were **DETERMINED** to solve them. We started with the first riddle, reading it over again carefully.

"So, first we need to find a mountain," Colette said. "And then we need to go where **blue** and **yellow** waters flow. Hmm. Could that be a river? Rivers have water that flows."

"And we'll meet some **SUSPICIOUS** creatures, but it doesn't sound like they're the ones who are stealing the lotus flowers," Violet mused.

Paulina nodded. "Right. The riddle says that the **GUILTY** ones are beautiful damsels."

I frowned. "Maybe the tanuki is just trying to **confuse** us."

Did the tanuki tell the truth?

"Well, telling riddles is in his nature," Will reminded me. "But I think there is **truth** in them."

"And what about the beautiful damsels? Have you heard of them?" Colette asked.

Will shook his head. "No. We'll have to ask for **information** as we go."

"But the riddles make it seem like we shouldn't trust anybody," Paulina pointed out.

"I don't think we have a choice," I said. "I think we should start by finding the 'ROUNDED MOUNTAIN PEAK' in the riddle."

"That's one way to do it," Will said. "But then there's the second riddle."

"It talks about a ruler who lives in the **sea**," said Paulina, "who can't stand anything that grows on land."

Violet looked thoughtful. "Flowers grow on land . . ."

"Yes! Like the **LOTUS FLOWER**!" Nicky cried. "So maybe this creature with the **three fins** is the one who's destroying them."

"Great **thinking**, agents!" Will complimented them. "Sounds like you've **SOLVED** the second riddle."

"So does that mean we should go to the **ocean**, and not the mountains?" Colette asked.

"That's the problem," I said, "because the first riddle implies that the beautiful damsels are the ones responsible for the **VANISHING** flowers. I think we need to **split up** so we can explore both paths."

I normally don't like the idea of splitting up on an adventure — especially in a **STRANGE** land like this one. The Thea Sisters didn't look too happy with the idea, either. Nobody said anything for a moment.

Then a ***cold wind*** started to blow. I knew we would have to make a decision soon and get moving, or we'd **freeze** in the Sakura Forest!

ADVENTURE COMES TO A CROSSROAD

Will shivered and looked at the clouds with a worried expression. I decided to take ACTION.

"We need to hurry," I said. "If all of the lotus flowers **VANISH**, this land could come to real harm. We should split up and get going."

"Agreed," said Will.

"But are you sure that's **safe**?" Violet asked.

"We'll be okay," Pam said confidently. "Let's form two **groups** and get out of here."

"I have an idea," Will

Here are our two groups.

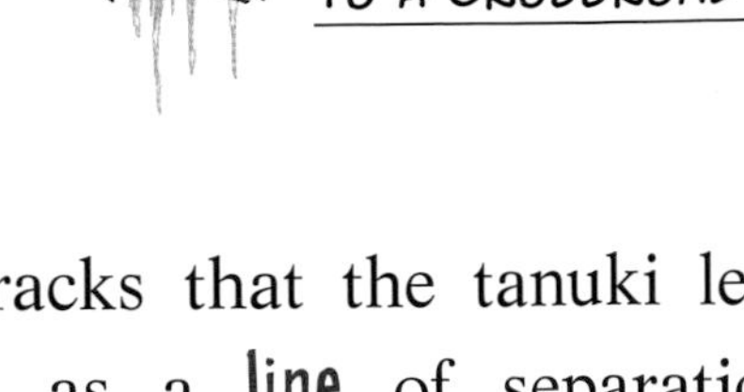

said. "See the tracks that the tanuki left? We'll use those as a line of separation. Whoever is on this side will come with me, and everyone on the other side will go with Thea."

I looked down at the snow. The footprints left by the tanuki DIVIDED us as evenly as possible: Colette, Pam, and Paulina were on Will's side, and Nicky and Violet were with me.

"**PERFECT!**" I said.

"Then let's choose where to go," Will continued. "I'll take my group to the mountain to search for the damsels."

"And we can look for the **sea**," I said.

"But which way is it?" Paulina asked.

Just then I remembered something the tanuki had said: *"Just open your eyes and look ahead!"*

I looked in the direction the tanuki had traveled, and that's when I saw the TREE. It was smack in the middle of the path ahead of us, and it had two big **BRANCHES**. They were each pointing in a different direction, kind of like a letter *T*.

"I think that tree is pointing to our two different **paths**," I said, motioning to it.

"But which way goes to the river and the **MOUNTAIN**, and which way goes to the sea?" Violet asked.

Pam scanned the horizon. "I think I can see the top of a mountain in the distance, and the left tree branch is POINTING that way."

"Are you sure it's a mountain? The snow could be creating a MIRAGE," Nicky pointed out. "It's like sand. It can make you see things that don't exist."

Two paths!
But which do we follow?

"But it's our only clue," Will said. "So my group will follow the **LEFT** path."

"And our group will follow the **RIGHT** path, and hope it leads to the ocean," I said.

"Where will we meet up?" Colette asked.

"Well, if we're all successful in figuring out this **mystery**, we'll all end up in the same place, won't we?" I guessed.

Everyone nodded.

"Right!" "Right!" "Right!" "Right!" "Right!"

Then we said good-bye and each group went down its own path. It wasn't easy splitting up, but in our **hearts** we knew we would find one another again.

IN THE FLAP OF A WING

Colette, Pam, and Paulina followed Will down the path on the left. It led them to an **ICY** plain. Their only point of reference was the rounded mountain **PEAK** in the distance.

Will took the **compass** out of his jacket pocket.

"It doesn't work!" he exclaimed.

Paulina frowned. "Something must be **interfering**."

"We'll just have to trust our eyes, and the **nature** around us," Colette suggested.

They agreed that was a good plan, and they marched on in the direction of the mountain.

Pam shivered as an **icy wind** whipped across the landscape. "Brrr! Even my fur has goose bumps!" She brushed some **snowflakes** off her jacket

They walked on, and the path led them to a round, snow-covered quarry with **ROCK WALLS** on both sides.

"It's a **canyon**!" Paulina said, and her voice bounced off the rock.

Colette looked around **cautiously**. "Something about this place gives me a **funny feeling**."

"Then let's keep **WALKING** until we get to the other —" Will started to say, but he **STOPPED** talking when he felt something brush the top of his head. He ***QUICKLY*** looked up, but all he saw was a dark **SHADOW** that soared up into the sky.

"What was that?" asked Colette, jumping a little.

"It kind of looked like a big BIRD," suggested Pam.

"It moved so FAST that we couldn't get a good look at it," Paulina observed.

They all stared at the sky, and something SWOOPED down on them again. This time, they saw they weren't dealing with an ordinary bird.

The creature flying at them had two ruby-colored wings, but also two arms and legs. It had a POINTY nose instead of a beak, and flowing white hair on its head.

The creature flew down and perched on a snow-covered rock in front of Will and the mouselets. Several others were nearby.

"Hello!" Will called out to them in a friendly tone.

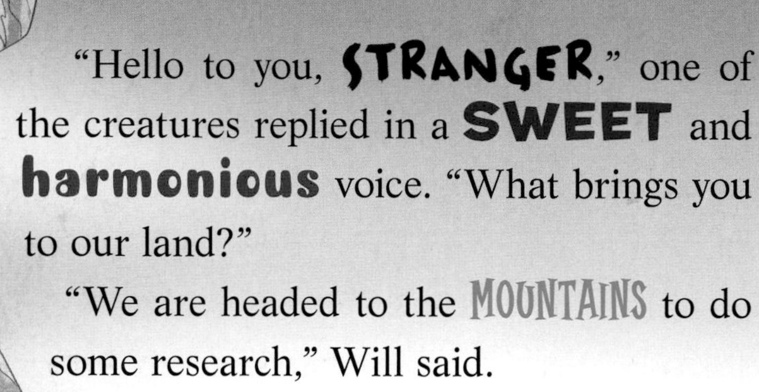

“Hello to you, **STRANGER**,” one of the creatures replied in a **SWEET** and **harmonious** voice. “What brings you to our land?”

“We are headed to the MOUNTAINS to do some research,” Will said.

Colette, Pam, and Paulina exchanged surprised glances, but they didn't say anything. It was clear that Will didn't know if he could **trust** these creatures yet.

"My name is Kunihiko. We are the **TENGU**, and we will help you," said the

creature. A musical sound came from his throat, and three other creatures swooped over.

Before Will and the others knew what was happening, a tengu grabbed each one of them and then took off in FLIGHT. Soon they were soaring across the BLUE SKY, with no idea where they were headed, and totally helpless in the hands of these StRange creatures.

"Where are you taking us?" Will asked, but none of the tengu answered him.

Pam was frightened. "Let me down, you big bird!" she called up to the tengu carrying her, but the creature just grinned down at her.

Colette and Paulina didn't try to RESIST. They knew they had no choice but to trust the tengu, and for some reason, they didn't feel any threat from them.

Where are you taking us?

Once they relaxed, they were able to enjoy the flight. They looked down as the beautiful LANDSCAPE of the Land of Minwa unfolded beneath them.

They saw snowy plains, lush forests, and **tall** mountains. Behind them sparkled the silvery mirror of the sea where Nicky, Violet, and I were headed.

The freezing air ***WHIPPED*** by them as they flew through the air, held by the tengu. Pam was sure that the tengu would drop them at any moment. But that's not what happened. The winged creatures **firmly** held on to them until they reached a forest.

This didn't look like the Sakura Forest — it had very tall *pine trees*, and oddly, they weren't covered in snow.

Will was about to ask the tengu why there was no snow on the branches, but then he saw the reason for himself. As they passed over the tops of the trees, he saw the branches flatten against the tree trunks, almost like an UMBRELLA closing. Then the trees spun around, and the branches opened up again, extending out like a ballerina's tutu.

"I get it," said Will. "The snow can't settle on the branches if they're constantly moving!"

Then one of the tengu let out a long, SHARP cry. The trees suddenly stopped moving. The tengu descended down into the stand of dense pines and carefully placed Will and the Thea Sisters down on a soft layer of grass.

"Welcome to the Forest of the Dancing Pines," Kunihiko said.

Will, Pam, Colette, and Paulina looked around in stunned silence.

THE SECRETS OF THE TENGU

The Forest of the Dancing Pines was a marvelous place.

A strong SCENT of pine filled the air. The fresh and pungent aroma mixed with the earthy smell of the rich soil on the forest floor, giving ENERGY to anyone who breathed it in.

Then there were the TREES. They towered high above, and their large roots sank into the soft and mossy ground that blanketed the forest floor. Small, delicate flowers grew at the base of the trees, and brown pinecones hung from the branches like ornaments.

Pam looked up, and could see a few pieces of BLUE SKY poking through the pine branches. Blades of light cut through the trees, creating beautiful SHADOWS on the ground.

"Come with me," said Kunihiko, and Will, Pam, Colette, and Paulina followed him.

"This place really seems ENCHANTED," Paulina commented.

"It's more magical than a cheese factory," Pam agreed. "Which reminds me — we haven't eaten in a while."

Colette gazed up at the trees. "They aren't moving."

"They only dance when someone approaches,"

Kunihiko explained. "It is a way to make the forest **IMPENETRABLE** to everyone but us."

Will kept silent. He kept wondering if these tengu were the **"suspicious"** creatures in the tanuki's riddle.

"Where are you taking us?" he asked after a while.

"You said you wanted to study this world," Kunihiko replied. "So we are opening our home to you. Unless, of course, you have **LIED** to us, and are here for some other reason."

He turned and stared at Will, his black eyes **GLEAMING**.

"Of course not," Will said quickly. "We are **happy** to study your forest."

They moved on in silence through the trees. Then Pam stopped suddenly.

"**Holey cheese**! It's beautiful!" she cried.

It's beautiful!

The trees opened up to a clearing in the woods. Small HOUSES were built right into the trunks of the surrounding trees.

"This is the WINGED VILLAGE, our home," Kunihiko said, pointing to the houses.

They watched, amazed, as the villagers flew across the trees from house to house.

"The tree trunks are tall and SLIPPERY, so our dwellings are safe from everyone who can't fly," Kunihiko explained.

Pam sniffed the air. "What a nice smell. It's so sweet and gentle . . . but it's intense, too."

Kunihiko nodded. "What you smell is the aroma of an **infusion**," he explained. "We tengu know how to prepare very special infusions and teas. Come, let us show you!"

Before they could react, Kunihiko picked up Pam, and other tengu picked up Will,

Colette, and Paulina. They **FLEW UP** and deposited their guests on the balcony of one of the houses.

There, they found a tengu who was grinding up some **green sludge** in a clay bowl — Paulina knew it was a mortar, a vessel used for grinding up herbs.

"Hello, strangers! My name is Kanjiro," he said, stopping his work to greet them. Then he noticed their **curious** looks.

"It's tree sap," he said, nodding toward the sludge. "It is an important **ingredient** in this infusion."

What a nice smell!

Kanjiro reached for a teapot and poured out a small, steaming **CUP** of the infusion for each of them. "Taste it. It's very good."

They all tried it — even Will, who was too **tired** and thirsty to be cautious.

Soon, however, everyone began to feel **strange**.

"Now you can tell us why you are really here," Kanjiro said.

"What do you mean?" Will asked.

"It's the infusion," he replied. "Everyone who drinks it must **tell the truth**."

"You tricked us!" Colette exclaimed.

"We don't have **bad** intentions," Kanjiro said calmly. "We just want to know what you are looking for. These are hard times here in the Land of Minwa, and you can't trust anyone."

"We are here for the **LOTUS FLOWERS**," Will blurted out, thanks to the truth infusion.

Kanjiro and Kunihiko exchanged **worried** glances.

"Not to steal them! We want to know why they are disappearing," Colette said quickly.

"We want to know, too," said Kunihiko. "The lotus flowers are very **IMPORTANT** to us. It is because of them that we can **fly**."

Will and the Thea Sisters looked amazed.

"It is a **LONG STORY**, but we will share it with you if you like," Kunihiko said. "It began long ago. . . ."

IN FLIGHT ONCE MORE

Will, Pam, Colette, and Paulina listened **intently** as Kunihiko told the story.

"Long ago, we tengu were able to **fly** without the help of the lotus flower," he began. "We were experts at making infusions from plants and flowers, but we used them for simpler things, such as healing."

Some of the other **TENGU** flew down to listen.

"May I join in?" asked one.

Kunihiko nodded. "Certainly, Naoki."

Naoki cleared his throat. "Things were **simple** — until some of us, **jealous** of the food eaten by the other forest creatures, became tired of our lifestyle."

"So," Kunihiko interrupted, "the tengu began to take food from other creatures. One day, some tengu were caught robbing **CHERRIES** from a distracted tanuki."

Naoki continued. "None of the tengu had ever ***stolen*** anything before, nor had they committed any crimes before that moment. The High Council of Winged Ones held a meeting and decided to IMPRISON the guilty ones in a **cage** until they had repented for what they had done. Meanwhile, the others who had TASTED the stolen food found that it had a tragic effect. Their wings turned from **red** to PALE and they forgot how to fly."

"What a **SAD** story!" Pam remarked.

Kunihiko nodded. "Our lives changed forever. We were forced to build **STAIRS** to reach our houses, and cover them with a

blanket of leaves to camouflage them."

"But how did you begin FLYING again?" Colette asked.

"Thanks to the lotus flowers!" Kunihiko replied. "One of our wise elders knew that the flower had very special properties, and he created an INFUSION to help us to fly."

"So you can only fly if you drink the LOTUS FLOWER infusion?" Colette asked.

Kunihiko shook his head. "The infusion can't do it all by itself! In order for it to work, we must believe in ourselves and free our hearts and minds."

"That's amazing," Colette said, her BLUE eyes wide.

"But it's true," said Kunihiko. "You can't fly with wings alone. You need **heart**, too."

"Unfortunately," Naoki continued, "now someone is **DESTROYING** the lotus flowers. We have some saved up, but soon we will run out and won't be able to fly anymore!"

"***That's terrible!***" Paulina exclaimed.

"Maybe we can help you," Colette said. "You said that you must **believe** in yourself with all your heart if you want to fly, right?"

"Exactly," Kunihiko replied.

Colette suddenly looked very thoughtful. "That sounds **familiar**, but I can't quite put my paw on it . . ."

"Maybe you're thinking of something you learned in the accelerated learning course," Violet suggested.

Colette's eyes lit up. "That's it! Thanks, Vi!" She continued:

"The pines have a message for you to treasure, to bring strength and courage beyond measure."

Everyone looked curiously at her.

"It's an ancient poem," Colette said, excited. "It's all coming back to me now. And I think it holds the key to your problem! It's called . . .

The Secret Poem of the Air."

Kunihiko was astounded. "This poem is from the history of our people. We thought the verses were lost forever. How did you know it?"

Colette smiled. "We have a few little secrets of our own."

Then she began to recite the poem.

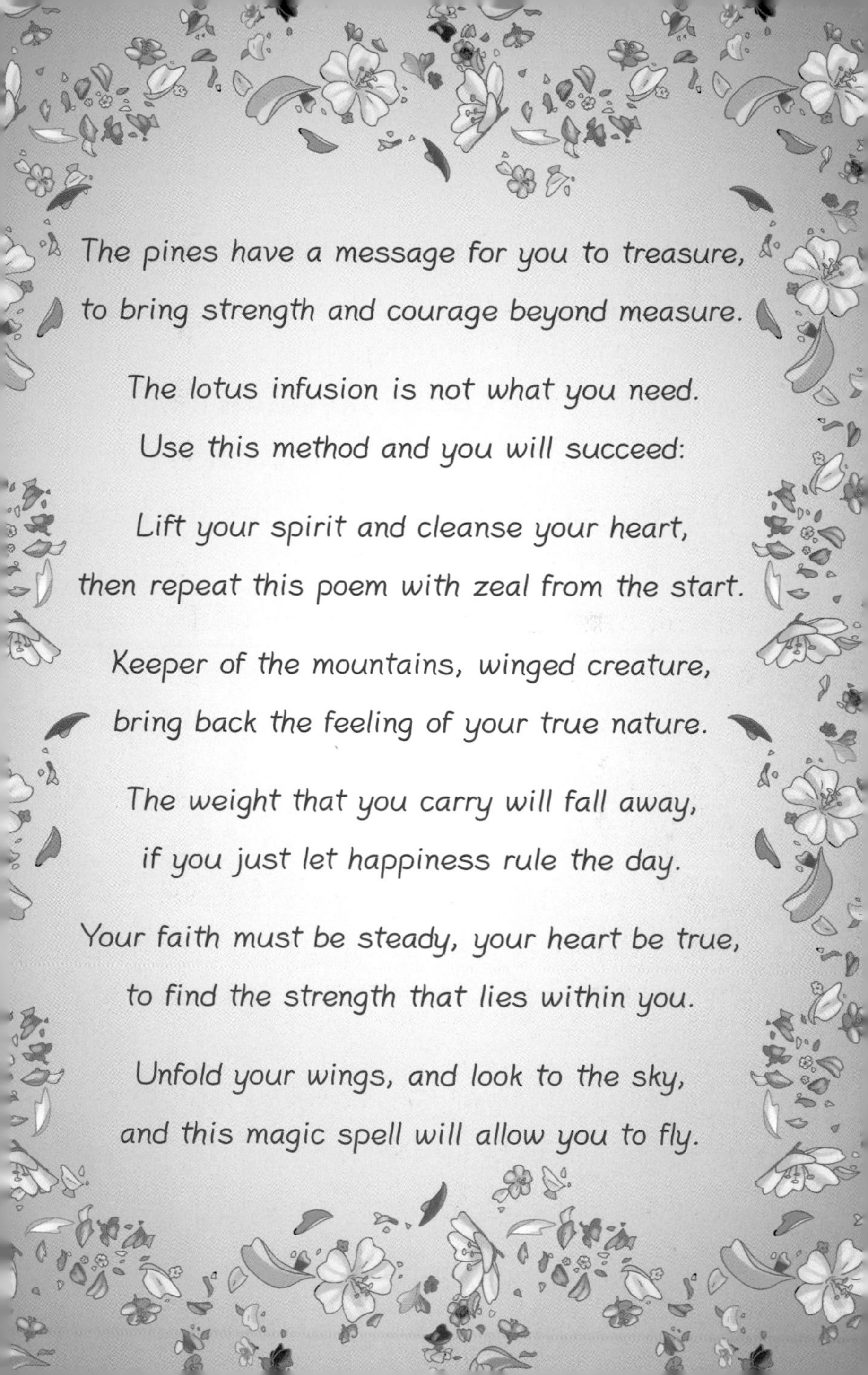

The pines have a message for you to treasure,
to bring strength and courage beyond measure.

The lotus infusion is not what you need.
Use this method and you will succeed:

Lift your spirit and cleanse your heart,
then repeat this poem with zeal from the start.

Keeper of the mountains, winged creature,
bring back the feeling of your true nature.

The weight that you carry will fall away,
if you just let happiness rule the day.

Your faith must be steady, your heart be true,
to find the strength that lies within you.

Unfold your wings, and look to the sky,
and this magic spell will allow you to fly.

"Good job, Colette!" said Paulina. "Now they just have to test it out."

Pam frowned. "But Kunihiko and Naoki have already had **LOTUS INFUSION** today, so it wouldn't be a true test," she pointed out.

Kanjiro stood up. "I never drink the lotus

infusion," he said. "I stay in the village to protect it and study **HERBS**, and have no need to fly. I will test the poem."

Kanjiro walked to the edge of the platform. Everyone watched, **BREATHLESS**, as he recited the poem. He flapped his wings once,

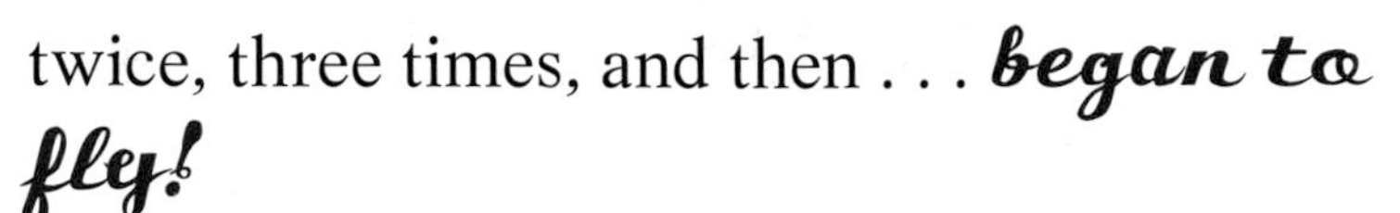

twice, three times, and then . . . ***began to fly!***

"I'm flying!" Kanjiro exclaimed as he soared through the **BLUE SKY**. "And without the help of the lotus flower!"

Inspired, the other tengu followed him. They recited the verses and then leapt into flight.

"Thank you, friends," Kanjiro said, after he landed next to Will, Colette, Pam, and Paulina. "You have taught us something so **precious**. We must return the favor."

A CLUE THAT LEADS TO SNOW

"Thanks to you, we can **fly** again without the lotus flower," Kunihiko said with a bow.

Kanjiro continued, "Tell us about your **MISSION** and what we can do to assist."

Will nodded. "We are trying to find out why the lotus flower is **DISAPPEARING**. We thought you might be responsible."

"Of course not!" Kanjiro protested. "We love the lotus flower, as you know."

"But we do have an **IDEA** about who might be doing it," added Naoki.

Pam thought about the beautiful damsels in the tanuki riddle. "Who?"

"They are fairies," Naoki replied. "They live not far from here, on the **snowy** banks of the CRYSTAL RIVER."

"A river? Does it have BLUE and YELLOW water, by any chance?" Paulina asked, remembering the riddle, too.

"Yes! Do you know it?" Naoki asked.

"Let's say that we do," Colette answered mysteriously. "What are the fairies called?"

"They are the Snow Fairies," Kunihiko replied. "But you need to be careful, because they like to play tricks on strangers and make the path disappear."

"How will we recognize them?" asked Paulina.

"They have very light skin, and long, blue hair. They are very beautiful, and SNOW CRYSTALS decorate their clothing," he said. "But do not be fooled by their beautiful appearance. They can be very cruel."

"Their pretty hearts are as cold as ice,"

Be careful of the
Snow Fairies . . .

Colette said, reciting a line from the riddle.

Kunihiko nodded. "So true."

"But why would the Snow Fairies want to destroy the lotus flowers?" Will asked.

"Out of jealousy," the tengu replied. "The flowers are always beautiful. But everything the fairies touch turns to ice, so they can't enjoy the flowers."

"How STRANGE," muttered Paulina.

Kunihiko bowed. "We hope this is helpful. It's the least we can do for you. You helped us remember that true strength always comes from the heart."

Colette nodded. "We should all remember to never lose faith in ourselves."

"And if we do, the support of our friends can help us find it!" Pam added.

Kunihiko smiled. "Quite right. And now, the tengu have four more friends!"

THE BRIDGE IN THE FOG

Kunihiko and Naoki accompanied Will, Colette, Pam, and Paulina to the edge of the Forest of the Dancing Pines. Then they told them how to reach the river.

"Go down this road until you find a crossroad. Take the path on the **right**," explained Kunihiko.

"Thanks for everything!" said Pam.

"And thank *you*," the tengu said. "Now we can **FLY** like we used to."

They all said good-bye and then Will and the Thea Sisters headed down the road. They walked on and on, but the ***sun*** didn't seem to move in the sky. And the **FLAT**, WHITE landscape didn't seem to change, until . . .

"STOP! Don't take another step!" Will yelled suddenly.

"Wha — aahhhh!" Colette screamed, looking down at the edge of the cliff just inches from her feet.

In front of them was a huge rift in the land, with steep walls hundreds of feet deep. The WHITE FOG that formed between the rocks was the same color as the snow on their path.

"We were about to fall in!" Pam exclaimed.

"You saved us, Will," Paulina said. "Thanks!" Then she took out the map she was drawing and added the rift to it.

"I just got lucky," Will said modestly. "A moment ago, I saw a breeze ripple through the fog, and I saw that it wasn't snow."

"Kunihiko didn't mention this. He said we would come to a CROSSROAD,"

Colette remembered. "You don't think he was tricking us, do you?"

Will shook his head. "I don't think so. He seemed GENUINELY grateful that we had helped him."

"We might just have missed the crossroad in all this snow," Paulina pointed out.

"So what do we do now?" Colette asked.

"Maybe we should turn back and look for a fork in the road," Pam suggested. "It's not like we can go forward, anyway."

"Let's look around here first," Will suggested. "Stay close together, and watch where you step."

The Thea Sisters followed him, paying careful attention as they walked along the edge of the cliff.

"I don't see any other paths," Will said with a frown.

Look out!
There's a bridge down there!

Pam looked over the cliff's edge. "Hey, there's a bridge down there!" she exclaimed.

They followed her gaze. They could make out the bridge, but all they could see was the middle of it. It seemed to be suspended in the fog.

They leaned over as **FAR** as they could, but they still couldn't see either end of the bridge.

? HOW WOULD THEY BE ABLE TO CROSS IT? ?

Will took a rope out of his bag and tied one end around his waist.

"I will go investigate the bridge," he said. "Please hold this rope **TIGHTLY**. It will support me if I fall."

THE GUARDIAN OF THE BRIDGE

Colette, Pam, and Paulina felt like their **HEARTS** were in their throats as they watched Will descend into the fog. Within seconds he disappeared into the milky **cloud**.

Below them, Will **CAUTIOUSLY** climbed down the side of the cliff. Finally, his foot hit a plank of WOOD. He'd made it to the bridge!

Then a strong wind whipped up, and Will heard a sound like a roar. He looked up to see an **ENORMOUSE DRAGON** with eight heads! Each pair of nostrils breathed out FIERY SMOKE. All sixteen of its **EYES** were as red as **FLAME**.

Will slowly stepped backward until he reached the cliff.

Aaaaahh!

"It's **OROCHI**," he told the Thea Sisters. "A dragon with eight heads and eight tails."

The dragon opened its eight mouths, breathing **FIERY FLAMES** that brushed against the bridge in a huge roar.

"Who disturbs my slumber?"

The dragon's eight mouths all thundered at once.

"Please excuse us, but we have to cross this **BRIDGE**," Will said politely.

Orochi laughed. "That's not going to happen!"

"But we **MUST** — otherwise we will have to turn back," Colette said bravely.

"That is your problem. I am

the **guardian** of this bridge, and you do not have permission to pass," the dragon huffed.

"What a nasty dragon," Pam muttered under her breath.

Will took a step forward, but the dragon aimed another burst of fire at him.

"One more step and I'll incinerate you!"

Will thought quickly. There had to be some way to negotiate with this dragon. But how?

Then Colette blurted out, "We are on a **mission** that will help your world! Please let us pass!"

The dragon **stretched** one of his heads toward her.

"Mission, you say? What kind of mission?"

Colette gulped nervously. She didn't want to make the dragon any angrier. But there was no turning back now.

"We know that the lotus flowers are

DISAPPEARING from this world," she said. "We are trying to figure out who is responsible so we can stop them."

The dragon didn't respond at first. Then he said, "I don't know anything about that. I only know that this is my bridge and you cannot pass!"

Everyone was thinking the same thing: what a SELFISH dragon! But no one dared to say it out loud.

"What do we do?" Paulina whispered to the others.

"I have an idea!" Colette answered. Then she turned to the dragon. "If you let us pass, we will give you something in return."

Orochi looked curious. "WHAT will you give me?"

"What do you want?" Colette asked.

The dragon thought for a moment. "There's

too much SILENCE in the middle of all this snow," he said finally. "I would like someone to **sing** to me. Like you, for example."

In one swift move, the dragon grabbed Colette in his **CLAWS** and then tossed her on top of one of his heads.

"*Let her go!*" Paulina screamed.

Will quickly began rummaging through his bag.

"*Sing me something! Come on!*" Orochi urged Colette.

Colette had never been a

good singer, and she was nervous, but she gave it her best shot.

"On top of a mountain, all covered with cheese . . ."

"You sound like a croaking frog," the dragon complained. "Can't you do better?"

"It's not easy to sing when you are the **prisoner** of an eight-headed dragon, you know," Colette snapped.

That's when Will found what he was looking for. He aimed a **FLASHLIGHT** right at the light of the dragon's eyes. The creature was used to being in dark fog, and, agitated, he shook his head and flew away. Colette fell, and Will caught her.

Pam and Paulina climbed down to the bridge. "Colette!" they cried, running to their friend. "Are you all right?"

"Yes, except my new pants are wrinkled,"

she complained. Then she called after Orochi. "You really are very rude, you know!"

Then they all noticed something. The dragon had stopped blowing SMOKE. The fog disappeared, revealing a blue and yellow RIVER below!

MUSIC SAVES

"The Crystal River!" Colette cried, pointing to the water running under the bridge. "It's the blue and yellow river from the riddle. The tengu told us that this is where the Snow Fairies live. And we found it!"

"We should cross the bridge now, before OROCHI comes back," Paulina said urgently.

But just as she said the words, the dragon circled back and flew right toward them. All eight heads looked angry.

Suddenly, a sweet music began to fill the air. Everyone looked around, confused, until they noticed a pink MP3 player connected to a portable speaker on the bridge.

"That's mine!" Colette yelled out, stunned. "It must have fallen out of my bag when I fell from the dragon, and the **radio** turned on."

The radio was playing a very **sweet** and beautiful tune.

"It's the **shamisen**!" Pam exclaimed. "The MUSIC we heard in the glass elevator."

"But how is it possible that the radio works here?" Colette asked.

"Yes, I don't think there are any **radio stations** in the Land of Minwa," Paulina added.

Will remained silent for a moment, then wondered aloud, "What if Colette's radio is picking up a *real* Japanese radio station?"

"But how?" asked Colette.

"The fantasy worlds and **real world**

are connected, thanks to the power of imagination, so there *is* a very real link between them."

"Thanks to MUSIC!" Paulina realized. "It's the same thing that allows us to travel in the glass elevator."

Suddenly, they all remembered the dragon. But Orochi no longer looked angry. He was PEACEFULLY listening to the music.

"Do you like this song?" Colette asked Orochi, and the dragon nodded.

She picked up the **MP3 player** and gave it to him. "It's for you, to keep you company."

"Are you serious?" the dragon asked, **SURPRISED**.

"Yes," said Colette. "But only if you promise, in exchange,

that you will not SCARE anyone who comes by here anymore."

Everyone waited for the dragon's response. Would he be **angry**?

"That seems like a fair pact," Orochi replied. "If I have **music** to keep me company I will be in a much better mood, with no reason to be SCARY anymore. So now you may pass . . . unless there is something else I can do for you."

"Actually, there is," Will said. "We are coming from the Forest of the Dancing Pines and we need to reach the blue and yellow RIVER at the bottom of this gorge."

The dragon nodded. "That is very easy. Once you cross the bridge, you will see a path that goes down to the river."

Paulina took out the **map** she was making. "I need to add the bridge, so we can find it again if we ever come back," she said, drawing quickly.

Will looked over her shoulder. "You are an **EXCELLENT** mapmaker, Paulina. We can use your skills in the Seven Roses Unit."

Paulina **blushed**.

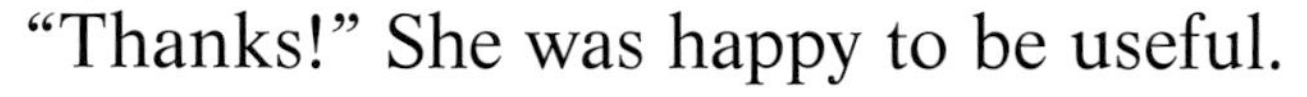

"Thanks!" She was happy to be useful.

"Well, **GOOD-BYE**, dragon," Colette said. "And thank you for your help."

They started to cross the bridge when Orochi called **LOUDLY** behind them.

"WAIT!"

Their hearts stopped for a moment. Everyone turned toward Orochi.

"I forgot to tell you," he said. "When you reach the river, you must **be careful**.

Often things are not what they seem . . . and not everything can be seen with your **EYES**."

"What do you mean?" Paulina asked.

But the dragon didn't answer. He just stared at them with his intense **RED EYES**.

"Maybe he doesn't want to tell us more, or can't," Will speculated. He called out to Orochi, "Thank you for warning us!"

The dragon's **eight heads** all nodded. "Be careful!"

Then Will, Colette, Pam, and Paulina left the dragon, as the sweet melody of the shamisen played behind them.

THE CRYSTAL RIVER

"This has been an **amazing** trip so far," Pam remarked as they headed down the **path** to the river.

"Absolutely," Colette agreed. "I can't believe I sat on the head of a **dragon**!"

"But we still don't know anything more about who is **stealing** the lotus flowers," Paulina pointed out.

"It may very well be these Snow Fairies. From all accounts, they're quite **dangerous**," said Will. He stopped and looked up at the sky. "**The sun is starting to go down!** We need to pick up the pace."

They walked quickly until they reached a snowy valley. The layer of snow underfoot was getting thicker and thicker as the path got closer to the mountains.

Then they heard the sound of running water, and the CRYSTAL RIVER was in front of them.

"We'll follow the riverbank to the mountains," Will said.

"Lead the way!" Pam said cheerfully.

As they followed the river, they could feel a cold chill rising up from the water. The surface was frozen in some parts, but the current was still strong, making a sound like leaves rustling in the wind.

"The pebbles on the bottom of the river are YELLOW," Paulina remarked. "Their reflection in the blue water is what makes the river blue and yellow."

It's the Crystal River!

"It's beautiful," Will agreed. "But I'm confused. Sometimes the river looks like it's curving, and sometimes it looks straight."

"That's funny, I noticed the same thing," Paulina said.

"Maybe we're just tired," Colette suggested.

Will frowned. "Let's keep our EYES open."

They continued along the riverbank, carefully watching each step they took. Then something strange happened. The sound of the running WATER suddenly stopped, and when they looked, the river was gone!

"How is that possible?" Paulina asked.

"Maybe we strayed from it," Colette guessed.

"We couldn't have," Pam said. "We were watching every step."

"This must be the work of the Snow

Fairies," Will speculated. "Remember, the tengu told us that they like to trick STRANGERS. Let's try to find the river again, and we'll be more careful this time."

They found the river again quickly, but minutes later they got off track and lost it again.

"How can we keep getting lost when we're walking so close to the riverbank?" Pam asked, frustrated.

"I suppose we could just walk right in the river, but it must be freezing," Will said.

"I have an idea," Paulina proposed. "What did Orochi say? 'Not everything can be seen with your **EYES**.' So maybe we should walk with our eyes closed. We will know the way by following the sound of the running water!"

"Good idea," agreed Will.

"Let's try it!" Pam said, and she began walking with her eyes closed.

The others did the same. A few minutes later, they opened their eyes, and they were still next to the river's path.

They hadn't even strayed a bit!

"It works!" Colette exclaimed.

"Let's keep going," Will urged.

They closed their eyes and started walking again — but this time, they couldn't take a single step forward.

SOMETHING WAS STOPPING THEM FROM MOVING!

THE SNOW FAIRIES

Paulina tried to lift her foot, but she was **STUCK**. She opened her eyes and almost couldn't believe what she saw.

She and her friends were imprisoned in large **BLOCKS OF ICE**!

"How dare you challenge us?" asked a sharp and curious female voice.

Two mysterious creatures floated above the riverbank. Each one was beautiful, with skin as **WHITE** as snow and hair as **BLUE** as the water in the river. They had to be . . .

the Snow Fairies!

"They tricked us, just like the tengu said they would," said Colette.

"Free us!" Pam demanded.

"What are you doing here? This is our river," the Snow Fairies asked, speaking in unison with chilling voices.

"Free us, and then we'll explain why we're here," Colette proposed.

The Snow Fairies burst out in icy laughs.

"You will stay here with us **forever**!" one of them threatened.

"Why? We haven't done anything to you!" Paulina objected.

"We are the **guardians** of the Crystal River, and we don't let anyone pass," the other replied.

Will and the Thea Sisters exchanged worried glances.

Who would help them?

"Let us go! We are on a very important **MISSION**," Colette insisted.

Colette's words seemed to interest the

Let us go!

fairies, and one of them spoke.

"My name is HIKARI," she said, "and this is my cousin, Hikaru. We have lived here on the banks of the Crystal River ever since we were born."

"We have a mission, too: to protect the Snow," Hikaru interrupted. "It is a precious resource, because the thick snow protects the seeds that are planted in autumn until they are ready to blossom in the spring."

"But protecting the snow is a big job for just the two of us," Hikari added. "So when someone passes through here, we imprison them and force them to help us."

"That's not very nice!" Colette cried out angrily. "You don't get help by force! We help out friends because we care about them."

Hikaru lowered her eyes. "We . . . don't

have friends," she said **SADLY**.

"Of course you don't. You **freeze** people!" Pam blurted out. Realizing how that sounded, she tried again. "I mean, you don't give anyone a chance to get to know you. If you hadn't imprisoned us in this ice, maybe we could have been **FRIENDS**."

Hikaru and Hikari exchanged looks of **dismay**. Then they turned back to Pam, Colette, and Paulina.

"Maybe you are right," they both said together, and at their words, the blocks of ice **melted**.

Well, most of the blocks melted — Will was still frozen!

"You are free!" said Hikari. "Now we can be **friends**."

"But you have to free Wili, too," insisted Paulina.

"But we are not interested in being *his* friend," said Hikaru. "Just you. He will stay here with us **FOREVER** and help protect the snow."

"No way! **FREE HIM** immediately!" Pam cried.

"We will not," the Snow Fairies said firmly.

Then Paulina **flung** her arms around the block of ice holding Will.

Everyone watched, **ASTONISHED**, as the ice melted until Will was free!

The Snow Fairies were bewildered. "You must be linked by true affection," said Hikaru.

"We ask for your forgiveness," Hikari added.

"The important thing is that we are free," said Will. "And now we can tell you why we are here. We are **INVESTIGATING** the disappearance of the lotus flowers. Many in the Land of Minwa think you are guilty."

Hikari and Hikaru burst out laughing.

"Us? Guilty?" asked **HIKARI** between giggles.

"What a SILLY thing for someone to think," said Hikaru. "We LOVE the lotus flowers, and would never destroy them."

"Do you smell the delicious scent?" Hikari asked them.

They all sniffed the air around them. A sweet and delicate aroma filled their nostrils.

"It's lovely," Colette commented.

"It's lotus flower," Hikaru revealed. "It is a rare and precious essence."

"We get this scent from the Ice Pixies," Hikari explained, holding up a small bottle of rosy liquid. "It allows us to find the way to our river even through storms and blizzards."

"Then who is destroying the lotus ver, if you're not doing it?" asked Will.

You will find some creatures farther up at

the mouth of the river. They are called the **kitsune**. They are the guilty ones!" Hikari and Hikaru said in unison.

Then a cloud of snow crystals swirled around Colette, Pam, Paulina, and Will, embracing them in an icy-cold hug. They heard two musical voices say "thank you."

When the cloud dissipated, the Snow Fairies were gone, hidden somewhere in the landscape of silent WHITE snow.

THE KITSUNE

Will, Colette, Pam, and Paulina began walking through the snow once more, following the river's course. The chilly air whipped against their faces, and the gloomy songs of owls accompanied their steps. But the landscape around them was enchanting, and the snow crystals on the branches of the pines created a beautiful sunset light show.

"Do we have a long way to go?" Pam asked. "I could go for some pizza about now."

"Well, we still haven't reached the rounded peak in the riddle," Will replied. *"To find the answers that you seek, look for a rounded mountain peak."*

"We may be close," said Paulina, pointing.

"Look at the shape of that **mountain**!"

The path in front of them became very steep, and it led to a mountain topped with a natural platform shaped like a perfect **CIRCLE**.

"You're right! Let's go," Will said. He attached his rope to the **VERTICAL** rock wall in front of them so that they could climb up the mountain.

When they reached the top, they found themselves at the source of the blue

and yellow river.

"How beautiful!" said Pam, and they watched the flowing water in silence for a moment.

"You know, I've been wondering," said Paulina thoughtfully. "The riddle says that the guilty ones might be beautiful damsels. Was it talking about the Snow Fairies?"

"Or maybe the kitsune," Colette guessed. "Whatever they are."

From the corner of his eye, Will saw something move behind a rock. As he approached, it ran off in a flash.

"Did you see something?" Paulina asked.

"I think I saw a FOX," he reported.

"Oh, no," said an unfamiliar female voice. "It was me that you saw!"

At that moment a very beautiful and elegant creature appeared before them. She held a golden sphere in her hands, and a

It was me you saw!
Hello!

soft fox tail waved behind her.

"Hello," said Will.

"Hello," replied the creature. "My name is Setsuko, and I'm a **kitsune**. What brings you to these parts?"

"We are researching a very precious flower," Will said directly.

"You mean *this*, I imagine," said Setsuko, pulling a LOTUS FLOWER from her hair.

Colette nodded. "We heard that someone is destroying them."

"**YES**, I have heard that, too," Setsuko said.

"Do you know who it is?" Will asked.

Setsuko's eyes widened. "I am just a kitsune," she said ***innocently***.

Pam groaned impatiently. "Can't you just tell us what you know?" she asked. "Some inhabitants of the Land of Minwa think that you kitsune are **destroying** the lotus flowers."

"I have heard the rumors," Setsuko replied with an injured sniff. "Many say that we kitsune **poison** the pond water where the flowers grow. But we would never do that!"

"Why not?" asked Colette.

"Lotus flowers are very special, even if they grow out of **mud**," explained Setsuko. "They remind us that it doesn't matter what our condition is. **EVERYONE** can make something beautiful and be helpful to others. Lotus flowers remind us of this, and they give us **courage**."

Everyone nodded thoughtfully. The kitsune had not seemed very helpful at first, but she was revealing herself to be **INTELLIGENT** and **SENSITIVE**.

Pam was still suspicious of the creature. She noticed that Setsuko seemed to be holding the golden SPHERE in her hand protectively. Was she hiding something?

"What do you have in your hands?" she asked in her direct way.

Surprised by the question, the kitsune JUMPED a little. She took a step backward but tripped, and the sphere tumbled out of her hands.

The sphere ROLLED right to Will's feet, and he picked it up.

Setsuko looked at Will strangely.

"You have obtained the sphere of my POWER. Now I am forced to help you!"

"What do you mean?" Paulina asked.

"I think I know," said Will. "The sphere that the kitsune carry with them is enchanted, because they keep some of their powers inside it. Whoever gains control of the sphere can force the kitsune to **HELP** him."

"Then let's ask Setsuko if she knows who is destroying the lotus flowers," said Paulina.

"I cannot lie to you," Setsuko told Will. "I am not destroying the flowers, but I know who is."

Everyone waited, breathless, for her to reveal the answer.

"It is Isonade, Lord of the Tides!"

"Isonade?" A look of recognition flashed in Colette's eyes, and she asked Paulina for a pen and paper.

"It's the second riddle," Colette cried as she wrote it out on the paper. "See, starting with the second line, the first letter of each line spells out '**ISONADE**'!"

IN ABYSSES IS WHERE HE HIDES:
IT'S THE GREAT AND EVIL LORD OF TIDES.
SOVEREIGN OF ALL, HE RULES THE LAND.
OH, TERRIBLE THINGS DOES HE DEMAND!
NAY, HE SIMPLY CANNOT STAND
ANYTHING THAT GROWS ON LAND.
DO START YOUR JOURNEY TO THE SEA.
EXACTLY THREE FINS ARE WHAT YOU WILL SEE.

Pam shook her head. "So we came all this way, only to be sent to the sea—"

"Where *Nicky*, **Violet**, and **THEA** are!" finished Paulina. "But how do we get there from here?"

Will turned to Setsuko. "Can you please help us find the **sea**?"

She nodded. "Come with me!"

So they followed Setsuko back down the mountain. She led them to a valley, to an offshoot of the Crystal River. They soon reached a jetty where a small WOODEN boat was docked.

"Board the boat, and keep heading downriver until you reach the sea," she instructed. "But be careful."

"**Good-bye**," Will said as he handed back the sphere, "and thank you!"

"Good-bye, and good luck!" the kitsune said with a **SMILE**, and she kept waving until the boat disappeared from view.

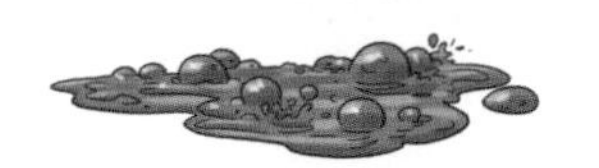

DANGER LURKING

While Will, Colette, Pam, and Paulina were off in the **MOUNTAINS**, Nicky, Violet, and I had headed down the path that we hoped would lead to the **sea**. We walked and walked, but all we could see was **snow**.

"Are we going the right way?" Violet asked, worried.

"I hope so," I replied.

Before long, though, the snow got THINNER and the air felt warmer.

Nicky took off her jacket. "We must be getting closer. **SEE?** There's a bunch of reeds down there. They grow near water."

We walked toward the reeds, and soon our boots got stuck in a thick layer of mud. Nicky pulled aside the reeds to reveal a quiet, **dark** pond. The surface of the water didn't move at all.

Suddenly Violet GASPED. "Look over there!"

Nicky and I turned to see where Violet was pointing, and I couldn't believe my eyes. Three STRANGE creatures were dozing under a big tree!

They looked like turtles with short, stocky **FLIPPERS** and heads topped with **tufts** of shaggy hair.

"Let's not wake them," I whispered.

We started to walk away, but I soon realized that my feet were **stuck** in the mud. Nicky and Violet were in the same situation.

"What's happening?" Violet yelled. She tried to move again, but only sank deeper.

"**It's quicksand!**" Nicky cried. "Don't move or you'll sink!"

I tried to stay **calm**. If we didn't find a way out of that quicksand soon, we would be in big trouble!

THE MYSTERIOUS KAPPA

"Take a deep **BREATH**," I instructed Nicky and Violet. "We'll get out of this."

"Do you need help?"

The voice behind us would have made us jump if we weren't stuck in mud. I turned my head around to see that one of the strange **TURTLE** creatures was standing behind us. I could see now that he was about half my height, and because of his webbed **FLIPPERS** he had no trouble moving through the quicksand.

Two more turtle **creatures** appeared behind him.

"Hello, my name is Takumi," the first creature said. "And these are my friends, Taiki and Daisuke. We are **KAPPA** and are happy to have you here. Would you like to visit our REED grove?"

"Yes, but would you mind pulling us out of here first?" asked Violet, who had **SUNK** into the sand up to her waist.

"Oh, of course!" Takumi cried.

The three kappa came closer, walking on top of the **mud** with their flippers. They grabbed us by the paws and ***pulled*** us out of the quicksand in just a few seconds.

"Thank you!" I said, with a sigh of relief.

"You're welcome," Takumi replied. "You've never been here before, have you?"

We shook our heads.

"I imagined as much," said the kappa. "No one who had been here would dare venture into the **DEVOURING SANDS POND**!"

So that's what that **TERRIBLE** place was

called! I promised myself that I would tell Paulina so that she could mark it on her **map**.

"What brings you here?" Taiki asked.

"We are on a **MISSION**," I replied.

The kappa looked at me with curiosity.

"What kind of mission?" asked Takumi.

Daisuke interrupted him. "Excuse me, Takumi, but they should wash the **mud** off themselves."

Takumi nodded and turned to us. "You must clean yourselves off! The mud from

the Devouring Sands not only **dries** your skin in an instant —"

"But it penetrates your soul and makes you **extremely sad**!" Taiki finished.

I nodded. "Frankly, it's not a very nice feeling. Where can we **WASH** ourselves off?"

"On the other side of the pond. There's no **mud** over there," Takumi answered.

Violet took a step, but stopped, wincing. **"OUCH!"**

"What's wrong?" I asked.

"My knee hurts," she replied. "I must have **twisted** it when I was trying to get out of the mud."

Taiki put an arm around her waist. "Come, I'll help you," he said.

We followed them to a flat rock on the other side of the pond, and Violet sat down. We all washed off the **mud** and immediately felt better. Then Daisuke approached, holding out a small jar.

"This ointment will ease the pain," he said. "Show me where it hurts."

"Here," Violet said, **POINTING** to a spot on her knee.

Daisuke opened the jar and spread the emerald-green ointment on Violet's knee.

"It's made from emerald grass, which helps ease INFLAMMATION and pain," he explained. "Just wait a few minutes before you stand."

Then Nicky got our attention. "LOTUS FLOWERS!" she cried, pointing to the pond.

As soon as she said it, the kappa quickly SPRANG into action, tying us up in green BRANCHES.

"So, you are here to STEAL our flowers!" Takumi accused.

"No, you don't understand!" Nicky protested as she tried to free herself. "We don't want to take the flowers. We want to find whoever is taking them and STOP them!"

"The lotus flowers are very important to us. We use them to make ointments like this one," Taiki said, showing us a jar full of blue liquid.

"What is it used for?" I asked.

"It is essential lotus flower oil, and it protects our delicate skin from the sun," Daisuke explained.

"But someone is destroying the lotus flowers, and we barely have any left," Takumi added. "We can't leave our POND anymore, because we cannot live for very long outside the water without the protection of the ointment. The air and the sun dry up our skin."

"So we started cultivating our own lotus flowers in our pond," Taiki continued. "But the flowers that we grow don't have the same power as the ones that GROW naturally."

"So you are not responsible for their disappearance," Nicky concluded.

Takumi shook his head. "Oh, no! For that, you need to look to the sea."

"And who should we look for when we get there?" I asked.

"UMIBOZU," Takumi answered. "He is the guilty one, for sure! He is a heartless MONSTER, and all the creatures in the ocean fear him."

Taiki and Daisuke began to untie us.

"We believe we can trust you," Takumi said.

"Thank you," said Nicky. "Now can you tell us how to get to the ocean?"

"Just keep heading east," Daisuke said, nodding in the direction. "But be careful . . ."

Violet stood up. "My knee is healed! Thank you all for your help."

"We are happy to help, and hope you solve the mystery of the lotus flowers," said Daisuke.

Then we said good-bye, and headed once more toward the sea.

THE SEA!

Violet, Nicky, and I walked for a while, and soon came to a FOREST of tall trees. They had BIG, flat leaves that made them look like mushroom caps. A **salty** smell filled the air. We were near the ocean!

"We are on the right path!" I said, excited.

"HOORAY!" Nicky cheered. "I wonder where the others are."

"Do you think they found that blue and yellow river that was in the riddle?" Violet asked.

"I am sure they are on the

right PATH," I said confidently. "And if Paulina is working on her **map**, it will be very helpful for us to understand the geography of this place in the future."

Then Violet noticed something. "Those trees up ahead are BENDING forward. That means . . ."

She ran off to look, and we followed her to the edge of a cliff with a beautiful view. We had reached the sea!

"Now we need to find Umibozu," Violet said. "Something tells me that won't be EASY."

"A boat would be helpful," Nicky suggested.

I looked over the edge of the cliff. "There are a few **boats** docked down there," I reported. "But it's a STEEP climb down."

Then I noticed something. "There's a PATH," I said, pointing. "Let's go!"

We need a boat!

We slowly made our way down the **STEEP** cliff, grabbing the rocky sides so we wouldn't fall.

The sandy ground was **slippery** under our feet, but the path was fairly short. When it came to an end, the beach was still several feet below us. We would have to **JUMP** down.

"I'll go first!" Nicky offered.

I knew that she could do it. Nicky is very **agile** and an expert climber.

She grabbed a rock that jutted from the end of the path, and then she looked for other holds until she was forced to let go. She landed on her feet on the **soft**, white sand.

Violet approached the edge and looked down.

"I can't! It's too high up!"

"Do what I did! Grab on to the rocks," Nicky urged. "And don't worry. I'm down here."

Violet grabbed on to a rock and then **JUMPED**. She kicked up a cloud of sand as she landed next to Nicky, who helped her up.

"Thanks, Nicky!" she said as soon as she was in the arms of her friend.

"That's what friends are for!" Nicky replied, *smiling*.

I jumped down next, and a **WIND** whipped up around the three of us as we walked toward the bay.

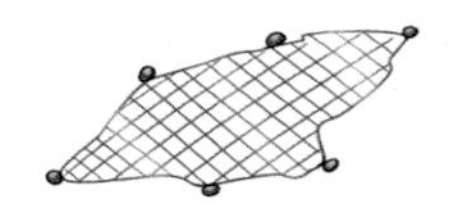

THE KIJIMUNA

We walked along the bay until we reached the **BOATS** that I had seen from the cliff. There were about ten of them docked at a small port. Nearby, we saw homes built on STILTS high above the big ROCKS at the base of the cliff.

The wind got stronger, and we HUGGED our jackets more tightly to us as we examined the boats.

"There's nobody around. That's strange," Violet said.

"Maybe because of the strong wind," Nicky said with a shiver.

Suddenly, I heard voices.

They were coming from behind a big rock.

I cautiously moved toward the voices, followed by Nicky and Violet. Behind the rock were two creatures with **THICK RED HAIR** and pointy ears. One was thin and one was chubby.

"What do you want?" the skinny one **snapped**. He didn't look happy to see us.

I noticed that they were making a FISHING NET. The skinny one was holding the part that was already made, and the chubby one was holding a shuttle with string attached.

"We are looking for a **BOAT** to rent," I replied.

"There are none. We only have fishing boats here," the chubby one said even more SHARPLY.

"Would you be willing to take us anyway?" Nicky asked, stepping forward.

The two creatures looked at each other and **sneered**.

"The ocean is **SERIOUS**. It isn't for strange creatures like you," said the skinny one.

"Oh, no?" asked Violet, **exasperated**. "Then who is it for?"

The chubby one shook his head. "You all are certainly very stubborn."

"We are doing important research," I said. "Please help us."

"And where would you like to go?"

Actually, we weren't sure. But if we told them that we were looking for UMIBOZU, they might not have helped us.

"I think we are in the village of KIJIMUNA," I whispered to Nicky and Violet. "They are similar to goblins and fairies. They are expert fishermen and they like to play pranks."

Then I turned to the two creatures. "We would like to go to the open sea."

"You are lucky, because we are leaving soon to go fishing," the chubby one said with a HUFF. "So you can come with us. But I will warn you, you must obey us once you are on the boat. Going out to sea is **NOT A JOKE**!"

"Thank you so much!" I said **warmly**.

But the creatures still did not seem to be warming up to us.

The kijimuna kept working on their net, and we waited in silence, not wanting to annoy them. Finally, the skinny one looked up.

"The sea has **calmed** down a bit," he said. "This is a good time to go. Follow us."

We followed them to the port, walking

past the stilt houses, where a CURIOUS face peeked out of the window to look at us.

Then we headed down the dock and climbed into a boat stocked with FISHING NETS and empty crates. The kijimuna motioned for us to sit on a wooden trunk, and we obeyed.

"Don't get up unless we tell you to, do you understand?" the chubby one ordered as he climbed in with us.

"IT COULD BE DANGEROUS!"

"We won't," I promised.

The other kijimuna put a second boat in the water, climbed aboard, and then began *rowing* vigorously. A moment later we headed out toward the open sea.

AMONG THE WAVES

We had been floating in the middle of the sea for a while when I noticed that the sky was getting darker.

"It's almost EVENING," I said to Nicky and Violet.

"Soon we won't be able to see anything," Violet said. Then she lowered her voice to a whisper. "How will we find UMIBOZU?"

"Maybe he will find us," I replied, but I wasn't sure how I felt about that.

The two kijimuna were busy fishing. They had lowered their net into the water and watched the colorful BUOYS bobbing on top of the water.

"Now!" the chubby one cried suddenly, and he pulled the net out of the water.

"Oh no!" he exclaimed, frowning. "It's EMPTY!"

"How is that possible?" asked the skinny one. "Something strange —"

Before he could finish, we felt something *smack* into the boat, rocking it.

"A giant wave! Hold on!" cried the chubby kijimuna.

We quickly grabbed the sides of the boat, and seconds later, it was hit with another **HUGE BLOW**.

The two kijimuna exchanged glances.

"Let's get out of here, and fast!" said the skinny one.

"Why?" I asked. "What's happening?"

"It's **UMIBOZU**! The monster of the sea!"

"He **CAPSIZES** fishermen's boats," said the chubby one. "We must flee!"

"We can't go!" cried Nicky. "He is the one we have come to see!"

The chubby one looked at us in **disbelief**. "You are here for Umibozu? You don't know what you are saying! He is a **DANGEROUS** beast!"

"It is very important for us to talk to him," Violet insisted.

"Oh, yeah? Then you will wait here for him **ALONE**!"

He jumped into his partner's boat and they rowed off in a ***hurry***, leaving us on that little boat in the middle of the sea with only an oil lamp. Alone!

ALONE!
ALONE!
ALONE!
ALONE!

Let's go back to shore!

THE MONSTER OF THE SEA

We were alone in the middle of the sea. We didn't know if Umibozu would **ATTACK** our boat again, or if we would be able to defend it if he did.

Violet looked at the sun dipping into the horizon.

"It will be dark soon," she said anxiously.

I was worried, too. The situation was getting complicated. Approaching Umibozu in the **darkness** could be dangerous.

"Let's go back to shore," I suggested. "We will find another way to reach Umibozu."

"Good idea," Nicky agreed. She started to row the boat when, suddenly, another ***blow*** shook us! It was much stronger than the last one.

"What could that be?" Violet asked.

All three of us had the same thought: **UMIBOZU!**

"It's him, isn't it?" Nicky asked.

"I believe it is, yes," I answered. "He is trying to **TIP OVER** the boat!"

"Soon he will succeed!" Violet added.

Something **smacked** the boat again, and a

wave of water poured over the side. Violet stood up impatiently.

"If it's you, Umibozu, stop hitting us!" she yelled. "We have come here to see you. We have to tell you something IMPORTANT!"

Nicky and I stared at Violet, admiring her courage. Then we waited for the monster's reaction. Seconds later, an ENORMOUSE dark and shiny SPHERE emerged out of the choppy sea. Violet stared at it, openmouthed, as the sphere swam toward us.

We had no idea what was coming toward us until a long TENTACLE poked out of the water. Then we knew: Umibozu was an ENORMOUSE OCTOPUS!

The tentacle whipped the air above the boat and landed on Violet's shoulders. She froze.

What was UMIBOZU going to do?

Umibozu!

Nicky and I jumped to our feet, ready to ward off an ATTACK. But that wasn't necessary.

"Who are you and what do you want?" the monster asked in a **DEEP VOICE**. We were scared, but the tentacle slipped off Violet's shoulders and disappeared back in the water.

"Umibozu, is that you? We were looking for you," I said.

"**It is I.** But were you really looking for me?" He sounded surprised.

Maybe he doesn't receive visitors often, I thought.

"Yes, we are here to talk to you," Nicky called out.

The monster seemed **pleased** to hear that. "Nobody ever wants to talk

to me. Nobody even wants to come close."

"Maybe because you SCARE everyone," Violet pointed out.

"But I wasn't always so ferocious," Umibozu responded. "I became this way!"

I exchanged SURPRISED glances with Nicky and Violet.

"What do you mean?" I asked, curious.

"Everyone got this idea that I am dangerous and cruel just because I am so BIG," he explained.

He really was gigantic!

I nodded, encouraging him to continue.

"Everyone avoids me, and many try to attack me!" the monster said sadly. "I got tired of everyone treating me like a FEROCIOUS beast, so I decided to become one. Why be nice to others if they aren't nice to me?"

"That doesn't make sense," Violet argued. "What counts isn't how others treat you, but how you treat them. A kind gesture spreads **goodness** throughout the world."

"While a bad act always has consequences!" Nicky added.

I agreed. "The worse you behave, the worse the situation gets!"

Umibozu was **silent** for a moment.

"You are right," he said. "Although I still don't know why you are here."

"We are researching the **DISAPPEARANCE** of the lotus flowers," I explained.

"I know who's doing it!" the octopus exclaimed. "It's Isonade, the **BLUE SHARK**!"

"But why would he take the flowers?" Violet asked.

"Because he is jealous," Umibozu replied. "He can't stand that such beautiful **FLOWERS** only grow in fresh water."

"So he destroys them?" I asked.

"Not on purpose," he answered. "He asked some **SALMON** to travel upstream and take the lotus flowers from the ponds and bring them to the sea. But then the **SALT** in the water destroyed them."

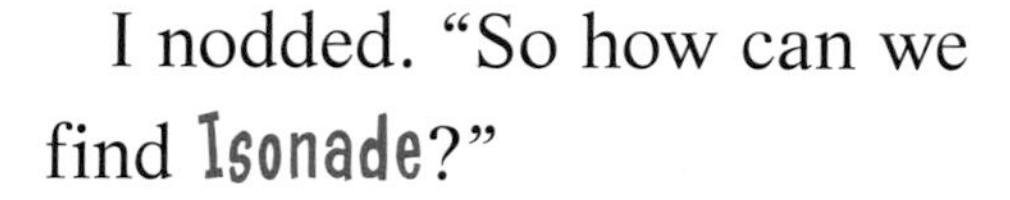

I nodded. "So how can we find Isonade?"

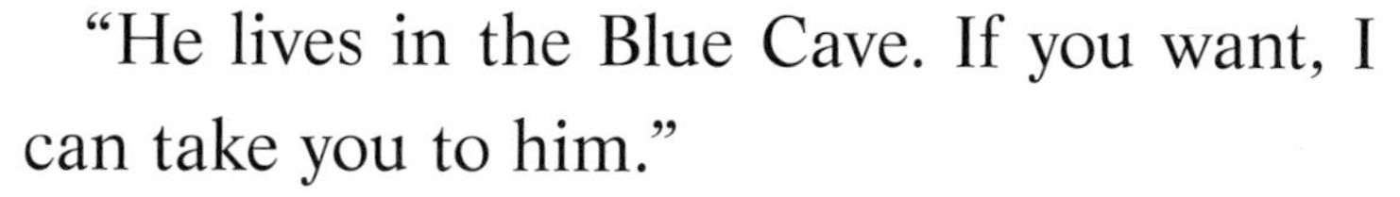

"He lives in the Blue Cave. If you want, I can take you to him."

"**THANK YOU**," I said. "You are very helpful!"

The grcat beast actually **SMILED** at us. Then he wrapped one of his powerful tentacles around our boat, picked us up, and swam toward the coast. I wondered if Isonade would be as nice to us. . . .

A NICE SURPRISE!

With Umibozu's help, Nicky, Violet, and I were speeding over the dark waters of the **sea**. We could see the shore in the distance. Then we saw something else in the faint evening light . . .

"**ANOTHER BOAT!**" Nicky yelled.

"I see it, too!" Violet exclaimed. "Maybe the kijimuna felt bad about leaving us and came back to find us."

So we asked Umibozu to bring us toward the boat. As we got closer, we could see . . .

four passengers onboard!

Nicky peered into the **darkness**. "I can't see what they look like."

The boat was heading toward us, too. Finally I could make out the shape of a

Hello!

rowboat, and I recognized the silhouettes of the rowers.

"**WILL!**" I shouted. "PAM! PAULINA! Colette!"

They all waved in greeting. We had found each other! How wonderful!

"Umibozu, could you please put us down?" Violet asked.

He gently lowered our boat to the surface of the calm sea.

"Isonade's cave is just in front of you," he said, pointing with one of his tentacles.

"You have been so kind to us," I said. "Thank you, Umibozu!"

"You're welcome," he replied. "I hope you are able to solve the problem and save the LOTUS FLOWERS. Good-bye!"

Then he submerged himself in a **whirlwind** of waves.

I held up the **lamp** onboard the boat to get a better view of the rowboat in front of us. Nicky rowed forcefully and we headed toward them.

"THEA!" I could hear Will calling.

Finally, we reached them. Our boats were close enough together that we could reach out and hold our friends' paws. How **wonderful** it was to see them and know that they were all right! Finding them was even happier because it was a surprise. At least for us, anyway.

"We were looking for you," Will said.

"How did you get all the way out here?" Pam asked.

"We had some help," I replied. "We would still be in the middle of the ocean if it wasn't for **UMIBOZU**!"

We were looking for you!
We're here!

Colette's eyes widened. "Umi-who?" she asked.

"Umibozu," Nicky explained. "He's a SCARY-LOOKING giant octopus, but he's very nice."

Nicky, Violet, and I told our friends about our **adventures** with the kappa, the kijimuna, and Umibozu. Will and the others told us about their journey so far. While we talked, Paulina got out her pen and started adding the names and details of our adventure to her **map**.

"So, Umibozu says that Isonade is the one destroying the LOTUS FLOWERS," I concluded.

"Isonade! That's who we're looking for, too," Paulina said. "We discovered that the tanuki's second riddle is about him. The **FIRST** letter of each line forms his name."

"So now we just need to find him," Will concluded.

"Umibozu told us he was a *great blue shark*," I said.

"And according to the riddle, he should have three fins," added Violet.

Nicky nodded. "Umibozu says he lives right there, in the **Blue Cave**," she said, pointing to the shore.

"**LET'S GO!**" Will urged.

I began to row the boat, leading the way. Nicky and Violet took turns holding the **LAMP**. The others followed behind us.

My mind filled with questions as I rowed. Would we find Isonade in the cave? Would we be able to save the lotus flowers?

Or were we rowing right into danger?

ISONADE, LORD OF THE TIDES

We **GLIDED** across the sea until we reached the Blue Cave. The cave's rock walls were an intense blue color, and the sparkling water created incredible tricks of light on the walls, like shimmering rainbows.

Right after we entered, we noticed a dark shadow moving in the water beneath us. It moved quickly, like a **black cloud** in a stormy sky. Then three dark fins cut the surface of the water.

"***Aaaahh!***" Violet screamed, grabbing on to Nicky.

"What was that?" Pam asked.

We stopped rowing and waited quietly in the peaceful darkness.

What a marvel!
Ooh!

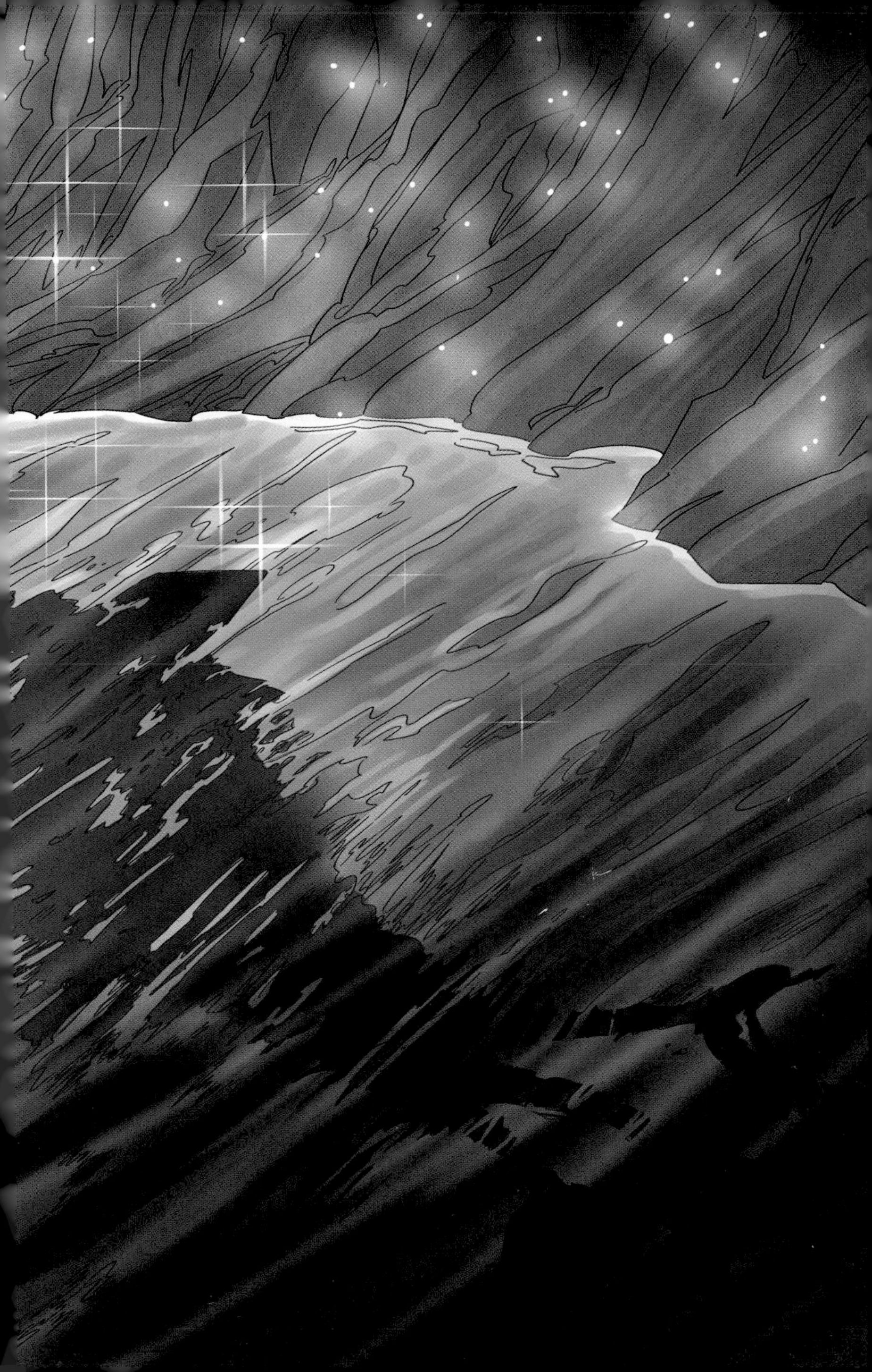

"Isonade?" Colette called out.

The fins reappeared a moment later, closer to the boat than they were before. They were blue, just like the rocks of the cave.

"Be ready," Will advised us, grabbing on to an oar. "In case he attacks."

"Who dares to enter my cave?" THUNDERED a voice from beneath the water.

"My name is Will Mystery. We are here on an important investigation," Will said bravely. "Are you Isonade, Lord of the Tides?"

"Of course I am! I am Isonade, GUARDIAN

OF THE DEPTHS. No one may disturb me!"

"What a nasty attitude!" Colette remarked.

Angered by the comment, Isonade smacked their boat with his tail, sending it skidding across the water.

"Don't provoke him!" Violet urged.

Will rowed the boat back to ours. Colette crossed her arms, but she remained silent.

We needed to act fast, before Isonade lashed out again. "Why are you destroying the lotus flowers?" I asked. But the three fins disappeared under the surface.

"Isonade?" Will called out.

"Why don't you answer?" Paulina asked. "Are you ASHAMED of what you have done?"

"I know NOTHING about the lotus flowers," the shark replied.

"So you haven't been stealing them?" I asked again.

A strange silence surrounded us. Suddenly Isonade SPRANG from the water into the air and over our boats, and then splashed back into the dark depths.

As he flew over us, we realized how large and powerful he was. He had three tails as well as three fins.

The water *churned* beneath us, rocking our boats.

"I don't want to hurt you, but I do not like to be wrongly accused," Isonade boomed. "I did take some flowers because they were very beautiful, and I was jealous that my worst enemy was enjoying them. But when I

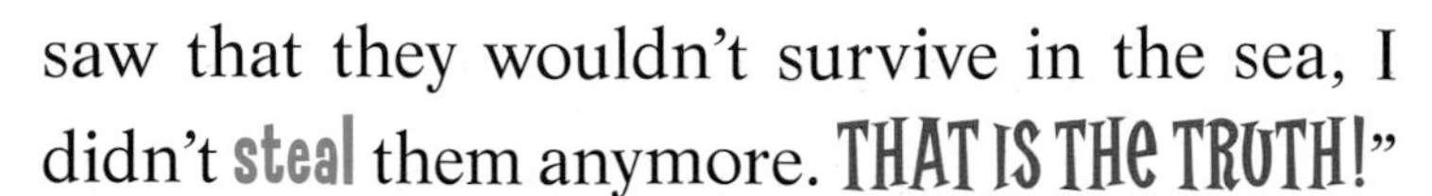

saw that they wouldn't survive in the sea, I didn't steal them anymore. THAT IS THE TRUTH!"

"Who is this enemy of yours?" Will asked.

"NAMAZU!" Isonade responded.

"Tell us a little more about him, please," urged Will.

"He is a giant catfish who lives in the Swamp of Lost Dreams, surrounded by beautiful lotus flowers," the shark said. "Once, Namazu and I were friends, and we lived in harmony on the borders of the freshwater and the salt water. But one day he changed. He became more and more nervous, and would get angry easily."

"Why did that happen?" Colette asked.

"I never found out," Isonade replied. "But I know that his fury can still be felt."

"How is that?" Will asked.

"With earthquakes. They are mostly

felt in the southern region. They also say that he devours hundreds and hundreds of pounds of **LOTUS FLOWERS** out of anger."

"What a senseless act," I interrupted. "Lotus flowers are **precious** for all the inhabitants of the Land of Minwa."

"**RAGE** can make you do senseless things," Isonade said. "In the end, your anger ends up hurting you more than others. But I am afraid that he hasn't understood that yet."

I nodded. "That is very true. You are a **WISE** creature."

"Would you like to know why I have **THREE** fins and **THREE** tails?" Isonade asked.

"Why?" asked Colette.

"They are a symbol of **BALANCE**," the shark replied. "It is the middle path where two enemies come together."

At that moment, a school of **VIBRANTLY**

COLORED fish surrounded Isonade. The water sparkled and projected a **rainbow** of color on the rocky walls. So that's where the colorful lights were coming from!

"Now I must leave you," the shark said. "Your mission is a just and courageous one. I wish you **GOOD LUCK**!"

Then he sank back down into the dark water.

"Please, Isonade, tell us how to reach the **swamp**!" Will called after him.

There was no answer from the dark sea. Then, seconds later, Isonade's three tails poked out of the water.

SMACK! The huge tails hit the water violently, and a tall wave sprang up. It picked up both boats and carried us out of the cave and into the dark **night**.

Hang on!
Heeeeeelp!

Someone is Spying on Us

The ocean waves must have lulled us all to sleep. I woke up to the sound of Colette's voice.

"It's so cold!" she complained.

I touched my jacket and realized that it was soaked. Shivering, I looked around. Isonade's wave must have pushed us all the way to the coast. We had floated into some sort of swamp, and the sun had already risen. The others were starting to wake up.

"What happened?" Pam asked.

"The CURRENT must have brought us here," I replied.

"Maybe this is the swamp where NAMAZU lives," Nicky guessed.

Where are we?

We pulled the boats to dry land. Then Paulina lit a **FIRE** and everyone gathered around to dry off and collect our thoughts.

"Isonade never told us where **EXACTLY** to find Namazu," Colette pointed out.

Suddenly, Nicky jumped to her feet. "I heard a noise!" she exclaimed.

"Maybe it's an ***animal***," guessed Will. "The light of the fire may have attracted it."

"Let's go check it out," Nicky said.

Will followed her while the rest of us stayed by the FIRE and waited. They reappeared a little while later, followed by a sort of tiny elephant with soft, striped fur on its **legs**.

"Here is who was making noise. He was HIDING in those bushes, spying on us," Will reported.

"It's a baku!" exclaimed Violet. "It's one of the things I remember from the ACCELERATED learning course."

"I remember it, too," Paulina added. "Baku EAT people's NIGHTMARES to make sure they have happy dreams."

"I see you are well informed," interrupted the baku. "Can I ask who you are?"

"First tell us why you were SPYING," replied Colette.

"I saw the fire and I was curious," the little elephant admitted.

He didn't seem dangerous, so I asked him, "Do you know a place called the Swamp of Lost Dreams?"

The baku looked surprised. "Why do you want to go there?" he asked.

"Because we are looking for NAMAZU and we know he lives there," said Will.

"I wouldn't do that if I were you," the little elephant replied.

"Why not?" asked Colette.

"Well, he's not in a good mood these days . . ."

At that, we heard a loud rumble and the ground began to shake. The tremor lasted a few seconds but it wasn't very strong.

"See! I told you he wasn't in a good mood." The baku looked scared now.

"How is it possible that a catfish can cause an earthquake?" asked Colette.

"Namazu is very large. When he hits the rocks of the Swamp of Lost Dreams, the vibrations spread throughout all the corners of our world," the baku explained.

"You need to take us to him!" I urged. "It's for the good of your world. We want to bring peace back to the LAND OF MINWA."

The baku looked thoughtful. Finally, he nodded. "I believe that you are telling the truth. I will take you to Namazu."

Then he trotted off, and we followed him.

THE SWAMP OF LOST DREAMS

By now the morning sun had **lit up** the sky.

Will, the Thea Sisters, and I followed the baku through the damp grass to the Swamp of Lost Dreams. The fresh morning breeze caressed our faces and **TANGLED** our fur, but it was a comfort after a night spent in the middle of the sea.

We walked through a stretch of land that passed through great **marshes** surrounded by swamp reeds. AQUATIC PLANTS with shiny leaves grew out of the water.

The baku had not said a single word since we had left. He seemed **worried**, and I thought he might be afraid of Namazu.

I hope we find Namazu!

Me, too!

Then the baku signaled with his trunk for us to follow him into the **THICK** of the swamp. The vegetation became denser and the plants were tangled up in one another.

"Does Namazu live here?" I asked our guide.

He nodded.

"And why is he angry?" Will asked.

"Maybe you should ask him yourselves," the baku replied. Then he stopped in front of a LARGE POOL of dark water.

"Namazu, you have visitors!" he called out.

He quickly ran off and hid behind a bush. Then the water on top of the pool began to **ripple**. An enormouse head emerged from the water. Two FEROCIOUS GOLDEN EYES looked at us curiously. We knew exactly who we were looking at.

We had found Namazu!

Why are you here?

NAMAZU'S STONE

Only Namazu's head was sticking out of the murky swamp water. He looked at us THREATENINGLY.

"Why are you here?" he asked in a sad voice.

Will took a step forward. "Namazu, you sound TROUBLED," he said kindly.

The catfish looked surprised. I guessed that nobody had ever asked him how he felt before. He rose up until half of his ENORMOUSE body was out of the water.

"There's a HOLE in your head!" Paulina exclaimed. We were all stunned.

"What happened? Are you **hurt**?" I asked.

"It is a sad story," said Namazu.

"Please tell us!" I urged.

"One time, a large stone filled this space that is now empty," Namazu explained. "It was a marvelous blue quartz! Someone stole it from me, and I want my stone back!"

"Who could do a thing like that?" Paulina asked.

"Someone who does not care about me at all, because I will die soon without the rock," Namazu replied **sadly**.

"Why is the stone so important?" Violet asked.

"It has **GREAT POWERS**," answered the big fish. "It bestows long life and serenity of spirit. I won't live for much longer if I don't get it back."

Then he roared angrily, opening his **mouth** wide. That's when Colette noticed something.

"Look! A **petal**!" she cried, pointing to his mouth.

"And it's from a lotus flower!" added Violet.

"So it's true. Isonade was right — *you* are the **REASON** they are disappearing," I said accusingly.

"So what if I am?" Namazu asked.

"You need to stop destroying the flowers," Colette said. "Don't you understand how **IMPORTANT** they are for your world?"

"I do," replied Namazu. "But the **LOTUS FLOWERS** allow me to live without the stone. I discovered that if I eat them, I am able to **STAY ALIVE**. But the more I eat them, the more I need, or they stop working. Soon there won't be any more left, and I will die!"

With that, the big catfish slipped under the swampy water.

I knew what we had to do next. "We have to find Namazu's rock to save him and the lotus flowers."

"How can we do that?" Colette asked. "We don't even know where to look."

The BAKU came out of hiding. "Maybe I can help."

"Do you know who stole the magic stone?" Will asked.

"I don't know him," the baku said, "but I saw him and I stole his dream."

"WHAT?" Nicky asked.

"Well, you know that I can eat people's BAD DREAMS so that they don't remember them when they wake up," the baku explained, and we nodded. "I can also steal all kinds of dreams if I want to."

"I could use you sometime," Pam said. "Especially the night before a **history test**!"

We all laughed, and even the nervous little baku smiled. "Well, I noticed the thief sleeping near the water, waiting for Namazu to emerge. I was curious, so I traveled into his dream. It was so interesting that I stayed inside it for a while. When I awoke, the thief was gone — and so was Namazu's stone."

"What was in the **dream**?" Pam asked.

"It was very **romantic**," the baku answered. "And it was a very unusual dream. Most dreams are like PUZZLES, with bits and pieces of things floating around. But his dream told a very definite tale."

"Please tell us!" Paulina urged.

So the baku began his **story**. . . .

On a crisp, clear morning at the end of summer, a young wizard was resting in a clearing high in the mountains. He lay on his back, looking at the sky and the passing clouds overhead.

Suddenly, a dark shadow flew across the sun. Shading his eyes, he saw it was a bird.

Was it a falcon? No, the color of its feathers was too light.

Was it a seagull? No, a seagull couldn't fly so high.

While the wizard was thinking, the bird swooped down and landed in a nearby bush. The wizard jumped to his feet and walked to it, but right before his eyes the bird transformed! It turned into a beautiful girl with long, dark hair and eyes the color of the sea.

The wizard knew she was some kind of magical nymph.

"Are you hurt?" he asked the nymph.

She seemed frightened, and responded with a trembling voice. "No . . . but where am I?"

"In the highlands of the Musk Mountains," the wizard replied in a gentle voice.

He helped her stand up. She was even more beautiful up close, and he knew she had come from far away.

"Where are you from?" he asked.

"I am a sea nymph, from the ocean," she replied.

The wizard was stunned. "How did you end up here?"

The nymph looked down at her feet. "I shouldn't have done it. My father forbade me from straying from our island. But every day I gazed at the mountains in the distance. They looked so majestic and mysterious, and I wanted to explore them."

He nodded. He, too, loved the beauty of the mountains.

"So I transformed myself into a gull to come here," she said. "I shouldn't have. My nature forbids me from straying so far from the sea!"

"It's the same for me," the wizard replied. "I would like to go to the sea, but if I leave this land, my energy will fade."

"So you understand me," the nymph said, and then her face turned pale. She felt very weak and far from home, and her strength was slowly giving out.

The wizard noticed this. "I will take you home," he said.

"But you can't come all the way down to the sea. You will hurt yourself!" the nymph protested.

"I will manage," the wizard replied, smiling. "Having you next to me will give me strength!"

And without another word, he held out his hand so that the nymph could lean on him, and they began to descend into the valley.

As they moved on, the nymph slowly became stronger while the wizard became more enchanted with her. They talked and laughed for hours, until the sun began to sink behind the horizon, turning the sky pink.

During their trip, something wonderful happened: They fell in love with each other!

Finally, they approached a bridge that led from the slope of the mountain to the nymph's island.

The wizard took her hand. "We could build a house on this bridge between your land and mine, if you will marry me."

"Oh, I will!" she cried, but then tears filled her eyes. "But my father will never let me. He wants me to always stay on the island."

"I will talk to him," the wizard promised. "I will convince him that we belong together."

She shook her head. "You don't know my father. He is a very severe man who never goes back on his decisions."

When they reached the bridge, her father was waiting anxiously on the other side. She ran to him and he greeted her joyfully.

"Father, this is the man who saved me," she said, leading him across the bridge to meet the wizard. "He has asked for my hand in marriage."

"And who is he to do so?" her father asked, furious. "Absolutely not! I will destroy this bridge if you ever dare to see him again."

The nymph gave the wizard one last, sad look and left with her father. But the wizard did not accept losing his love. He learned of a rock that curbed the soul of whoever possessed it, making their anger disappear: the rock of Namazu the catfish.

Then he set his plan in motion: He would steal the rock to calm the angry heart of the nymph's father, hoping that he would allow them to be wed.

THE BAMBOO FOREST

The baku finished telling the story of the wizard and the young nymph.

"How romantic!" Violet commented.

"That wizard must really like her a lot," Colette added.

"But he did a terrible thing, stealing Namazu's rock," Paulina pointed out.

"Sometimes people have good intentions when they do the wrong thing," I said. "The important thing is to fix it and learn from your mistakes."

"That's right," Will agreed. "And now we need to find this wizard. Do you know his name?" he asked the baku.

The creature shook his head. "There were

no names in the DREAM."

"So what do we do?" Nicky asked.

"Well, we could go to the Musk Mountains," Pam said. "But how will we know where to LOOK?"

"There might be someone you can ask. But getting an answer won't be easy," the baku warned. "There are seven little fairies who live in a TREE who know a lot about the Land of Minwa."

"But why do you think they won't help us?" asked Will.

"Because they RARELY ever do," the baku replied. "They laugh so much that they often don't even speak, or if they do, they forget what they were saying."

"Where is this tree?" Nicky asked.

"It's in the BAMBOO FOREST, about an hour's walk east of here," the little elephant replied. He showed us a **RED RIBBON**. "Look for red ribbons like this one tied to the tree trunks as you walk. And make sure you don't stray from the path!"

We thanked the baku and set off. We walked for almost an hour, leaving the sea at our backs and climbing the hills until we came to a stand of hundreds of thin, green trunks that formed a thick forest.

We had reached the Bamboo Forest!

We stopped to observe and admire the tall, SLENDER plants.

"This reminds me of the forests near my home back in China," Violet said wistfully.

"Look, there are many **paths** through the trees," Nicky pointed out.

"And each path is marked by a different-colored ribbon," Paulina observed.

I held up the **RED RIBBON**. "It's a good thing the baku gave us this. Colette, can you lead the way?"

"Sure," Colette replied, taking the ribbon from me.

So we **CAUTIOUSLY** made our way through the Bamboo Forest, following the red ribbons and being sure not to stray off the path. It was like walking through a **LABYRINTH**!

THE TREE OF FAIRIES

We slowly made our way through the BAMBOO FOREST. The ribbons were tied up high on the bamboo stalks, and our **EYES** were focused on them as we walked.

"Aah!" Paulina **SHOUTED** **suddenly**, as she tripped and fell **FORWARD**.

Will was next to her and caught

her before she hit the ground.

"Did you hurt yourself?" he asked.

"No," Paulina replied. "I was looking up at the ribbons and tripped over a twig. Thanks for catching me."

"No problem," Will said with a smile.

"I'm just glad you didn't fall into another path," I said, remembering the baku's warning.

We continued walking without any other incidents. The walk seemed much **longer** than an hour, and soon we wondered if we had somehow taken the **WRONG PATH**. But we were still following the ribbons . . .

Then a sharp little laugh interrupted our thoughts. It was followed by a second laugh, then a third, and then . . . many more! They were faint and happy little voices, but they got louder as we continued on the path. The

SNOW softened the sound of our footsteps.

Then the path came to a **THICK** stand of trees, and we pushed aside the branches. What we saw left our mouths hanging open in amazement.

A large JAPANESE MAPLE stood majestically in the middle of a clearing. Something sparkled in the leaves, casting **golden rings** of light around the branches. Then we heard the laughter again, and it filled the air all around us. We had found the Tree of Fairies!

As we got closer, we could see the tiny creatures as they ***fluttered*** among the branches. Violet stepped up to get a better look at them.

The fairies had **shiny** hair and sparkly wings that constantly moved. They appeared to be nice.

BUT WHY DID THEY LAUGH SO MUCH?

Violet thought she had an idea. Her grandfather had taught her that those who laugh a lot without reason often do it to get attention. She held out her hand, **GENTLY** grazing one of the little fairy's feet.

The fairy immediately stopped laughing and looked at her. The other fairies had the same reaction.

"Everyone comes here to ask you something, but they are never interested in *you*, isn't that right?" Violet asked.

"Yes, that's exactly right!" the **LITTLE FAIRY** replied.

We were speechless.

Can we do
something for you?

Violet had managed to win over the fairies with her **SENSITIVITY**!

"We are also here to ask you something. But first I want to know if you are happy or if there is something we can do for you," Violet continued.

The fairies looked at one another. The one who had spoken first said, "My name is Reika and I am a fairy. My friends and I are the **guardians** of the secrets of the Land of Minwa. The roots of our tree cross throughout this world and hear everything that happens in our land."

"That's marvemouse!" I exclaimed.

"Yes!" Reika agreed. "We just have to sit here on the branches, and we learn many things."

"But sometimes we would prefer **NOT** to learn anything!" exclaimed a red-haired fairy in a decisive voice. "Everybody asks us for help when something is wrong. But then they leave, and nobody ever comes back to **THANK** us or to say that they are **HAPPY** because of us."

"That's why we laugh so much," interrupted a brown-haired fairy. "So we can stay happy and not think about all the creatures who forget to say **thank you**."

"But you have listened to us," Reika said. "You asked us something about ourselves, and this has made us happy! How can we ***REPAY*** you?"

We told the fairies about what the baku had learned in the

dream about the wizard and the sea nymph.

"You are looking for Orihime and Hikoboshi!" exclaimed the red-haired fairy.

"Excuse me?" I asked.

"The name of the sea nymph is Orihime, and the wizard of the Musk Mountains is Hikoboshi," explained Reika. "He lives at the edge of the BAMBOO FOREST. You must follow the path of yellow ribbons to get there. You will find a LONG staircase, and Hikoboshi lives at the top. And remember this: Watch out for those who only follow their hearts!"

THE WIZARD HIKOBOSHI

We said good-bye to the fairies of the trees. As we walked through the Bamboo Forest once more, its fresh **scent** filled us with **PEACE**. We followed the path of the yellow ribbons to a chain of extraordinary **mountains**.

The slope of one of the mountains rose up in front of us, covered in a layer of **snow** as fine as grated cheese. The weather had improved, and it wasn't as **cold**.

"Look!" Pam exclaimed. She pointed to the top of the slope, where a house that looked like a small **castle** rose up from the rock.

A staircase ran up the mountainside.

"It's HIKOBOSHI'S house!" Colette cried.

"Let's get closer!" Will urged.

We walked to the base of the stairs. A golden bell hung from a wooden archway at the bottom. I rang the bell, and a clear TONE filled the air.

A man APPEARED at the top of the stairs and took a few steps down. He looked young and strong, with dark brown EYES and long blond hair. It had to be Hikoboshi.

"Good day. We are looking for Hikoboshi the wizard," Will said politely.

"You have found him," said Hikoboshi. "What do you want?"

"We'd like to SPEAK with you," Will replied.

The wizard shook his head. "I don't have time. Go away!"

"He doesn't TRUST us," Colette whispered,

What do you want?

and I knew she was right. He would never let us up the stairs.

"We have come for the **stone**!" I called out. "Namazu will die if he doesn't get the stone back soon. You must give it back to him!"

Hikoboshi avoided my eyes. "I don't know what you're talking about."

At this point I got angry. "I am sorry to tell you this, Hikoboshi, but you are selfish! Because of your action, the **LOTUS FLOWERS** are disappearing from the Land of Minwa. You are putting your whole world in **DANGER**!"

Hikoboshi did not respond. He turned around and went back into his house, slamming the door behind him.

"We should try talking to **ORIHIME**," Paulina suggested.

"But we don't know where she lives," Nicky replied.

Colette's eyes sparkled. "I know! Let's follow Hikoboshi. I bet that he will go and visit her soon. If he is truly in love, he won't stay far away from her."

"Good idea," Will agreed. "Let's **hide** down here and wait until he comes down."

So we hid behind some trees and waited.

"*There he is!*" Nicky exclaimed suddenly.

"Shhh! He can't find out that we're here," Colette hissed.

We stayed **hidden** from the wizard until he started walking down the slope, and then we followed him. He had a package in his hand. He turned around a few times, almost like he knew he was being ***FOLLOWED***, but we kept our distance. If he had seen us, our plan would have been ruined.

Soon he reached the sea, and we could see a small island out in the water. It was sprinkled with plain, well-built homes surrounded by well-kept gardens. A WOODEN BRIDGE linked the island to the mainland.

"It's the bridge from the baku's story!" I whispered.

SWEET ORIHIME

Hikoboshi began to cross the bridge that linked the land to Orihime's island. On the other side, we could see a woman **RUNNING** across the bridge from the other side. The two of them met halfway.

Orihime was just as **GRACEFUL** and beautiful as I had pictured her. She took the gift that Hikoboshi was carrying.

"My father is becoming more and more kind," she reported happily. "I think soon he will consent to our marriage."

Hikoboshi smiled. "Now go. We will meet again very soon."

After a tender HUG, they each turned and walked back to their own lands.

"Good. Now we must reach Orihime and talk to her," Will said as soon as Hikoboshi had gone.

We followed the nymph to a one-story house surrounded by a beautiful garden. Orihime walked inside, leaving the door OPEN, and we slowly approached the stairs.

Inside, the nymph was seated on the floor and seemed lost in far-off THOUGHTS. When she turned and saw us, she jumped with surprise.

She looked at us, confused. After all, we were **seven strangers** standing in her garden. I smiled at her. She hesitated for a moment but then came to meet us.

"Hello," I said. "Are you **ORIHIME**?"

"Yes," she answered.

"We are sorry to show up like this, but we are here on an **URGENT MATTER**," I continued. "My name is Thea Stilton, and my *friends* are Will, Colette, Pam, Nicky, Violet, and Paulina."

Orihime frowned. "What **URGENT** matter?"

"It is about the LOTUS FLOWERS," I replied.

Orihime nodded sadly and then invited us inside. She had us sit around a table, and I noticed Hikoboshi's package siting in the center of it.

Pam sniffed the air — the package was giving off a delicious scent. Her stomach made a quiet grumbling noise that made everyone smile.

"Would you like something to EAT?" Orihime asked sweetly. "You all seem very tired."

We gratefully accepted her invitation. I couldn't remember the last time we had eaten. Orihime put a kettle of water on to BOIL and then opened Hikoboshi's package. Inside was a basket of purple fruits similar to blackberries.

"They are enchanted blackberries, a special

fruit that can only be found on the Musk Mountains. My boyfriend gave them to me as a gift," she explained, blushing a little. "They are DELICIOUS. Please try some!"

As we enjoyed the exquisite fruit, Orihime served us some aromatic tea. She explained it was called amacha and was made from fermented hydrangea leaves. It was wonderful!

After the tea we told her the reason for our visit.

"The lotus flowers are DISAPPEARING from the Land of Minwa," I said. "But we know how to stop them from becoming extinct."

Orihime stood up and went to the next room. She returned with a clear bowl with something floating in it.

It was a lotus flower!

"Unfortunately, I know about the disappearance of the flowers," she said. "This is the only one that I was able to save. Do you know who is responsible?"

"His name is **NAMAZU**," Paulina replied.

Orihime gasped. "The catfish that lives in the Swamp of Lost Dreams! Why would he do something so **horrible**?"

"Because someone stole something that he needs to live, and if he wants to stay alive he must keep **eating** all the lotus flowers," Will answered.

"What could be so precious?" the nymph asked.

"It is a **BLUE QUARTZ**," I told her.

She brought her hands up to her face. "That is the stone that Hikoboshi gave to my father!"

"Yes, that's the one," Colette said.

"I know it is a **special** stone," Orihime said. "My father has been very calm since he's had it, and he has almost changed his mind about Hikoboshi!"

"Yes, the stone has a calming power over whoever possesses it," Violet explained.

"But Namazu can't live very long without the stone," Nicky added. "If he doesn't get the quartz back soon, he'll eat the flowers until they are gone!"

"I understand," Orihime said. "But I can't believe that Hikoboshi would do something like that. How could he steal?"

"Because he loves you, and sometimes when you're really in love you can make mistakes," I said. "But I am sure that he will understand."

Orihime nodded. "The lotus flowers are

almost extinct. We must not wait. The stone must be given back to Namazu immediately."

Without another word, she left the room and soon returned with the stone. It was **bright** and **beautiful**, and bigger than a basketball. She gave it to me.

"Thank you," I said.

"Now your father will forbid you to see Hikoboshi again," Colette said **sympathetically**.

"The **SAFETY** of the Land of Minwa is more important," Orihime said **sadly**, but with a determined look.

A LONG DASH

We said good-bye to Orihime and left her house. I handed the **HEAVY** stone to Will.

We knew there was no time to waste, so we raced back through the BAMBOO FOREST. First we followed the yellow path, and then the red one.

We were exhausted when we finally reached the Swamp of Lost Dreams. The baku couldn't believe his eyes.

"You did it!" the little elephant cheered.

"Call Namazu, quickly!" Will urged.

"Umm . . . Namazu?" the baku called out shyly.

The catfish slowly emerged from the muddy water. His once shiny skin was dull, and his eyes looked red.

"What do you want? Get out of here! Leave me be!" he said crossly. Then he sank back into the **dark** water.

"He's not feeling well," the baku explained.

"Has he eaten more flowers?" Violet asked.

The baku nodded. "Yes, he devoured every one he could find. But he always needs MORE!"

Will didn't wait for his return. He clutched the stone to his chest and JUMPED into the swamp, trying not to think about the

cold. When he reached Namazu, he put the stone back into the hole in the catfish's head.

On shore, we all waited anxiously for Will to reappear. We had faith in him, but he was doing something very DANGEROUS!

Finally, some air bubbles appeared on the surface and Will's snout POKED out of the water.

We couldn't tell right away if he had succeeded. But then Namazu jumped high in the air, and we saw the stone in place.

"Well done!" we cried, applauding. The big catfish leapt out of the water again, scooping up Will on his back, and brought him to shore. We helped our friend out of the water.

"Are you cold?" Paulina asked, offering him her scarf so he could dry off.

"Yes, but the important thing is that the

Bravo!

stone was returned to its rightful place, and that Namazu gets better," Will replied.

"Thank you for helping me," Namazu said.

"Now you won't eat LOTUS FLOWERS anymore, right?" Paulina asked.

"Thanks to you, it is no longer necessary," Namazu confirmed.

We all breathed a **SIGH** of relief. The precious flowers were safe now. But we still had **something** to sort out. What would happen to Orihime and Hikoboshi?

Namazu suddenly looked angry. "I want to know who **StOLE** my stone!"

We told him, trying to explain the reason for the **terrible act** that Hikoboshi had committed.

Namazu listened carefully.

"He put his world in danger for a nymph!" he said with contempt.

"But **love** is the most beautiful feeling there is," responded Paulina. "Maybe you don't understand because you have never loved anyone."

Those words **struck** the catfish like arrows and penetrated his hardened heart. He looked sad.

"Oh, but you are wrong," he said. "I have **LOVED** before. Thank you for reminding me what it feels like."

"Good job, Paulina," Will whispered. "You have a big heart, and you have softened the heart of this great beast."

Colette stepped closer to Namazu. "Would you like to share your story with us? Who did you love?"

"She was a beautiful catfish like me," Namazu began, "but our love was **forbidden**, too. One day she disappeared and I never saw her again."

"What a sad story!" Violet said.

"I am sorry if I reminded you of **bad memories**," Paulina said sincerely.

Namazu shook his large head. "No. On the contrary, you have reminded me how beautiful and important love is. So the *couple* will have to separate now?"

I nodded. "Unfortunately, yes. Without the stone, the heart of Orihime's **FATHER** will become hard again, and he will forbid their love."

NAMAZU was silent for a few seconds. Then he called out, "Baku? Take the **STONE** from my head, please."

We watched, puzzled, as the baku obeyed.

"Now break it in **HALF**, and give one half to me and one half to our friends," he ordered.

We were squeakless.

"Half of the stone is for the nymph's father," Namazu explained. "This way, ORIHIME can find happiness."

"That is so kind of you!" Paulina said, speaking for all of us.

NAMAZU HAD PERFORMED A TRULY WONDERFUL GESTURE.

"Will the stone work even if it is cut in half?" Violet asked. "And most important, will you be all right?"

"Yes, I will," Namazu replied. "Maybe I won't live as long, but it will **HELP** someone else live a better life."

Then he **PLUNGED** into the **SWAMP** and disappeared.

HAPPY ENDING

The Thea Sisters, Will, and I were thrilled. Orihime would be **so happy** to get the stone back and fulfill her dream!

"Do you think that **HALF** the stone will be enough to work on Orihime's father?" Pam asked, as we walked back to the nymph's house.

"I think so," Colette replied. "And he will be even more **CONVINCED** when he sees how happy his daughter is."

"Thea, what do you think?" Violet asked.

"I'm sure that everything will work out for the best," I said confidently. "I will talk to Orihime's father if I have to. The **love** between Orihime and Hikoboshi is strong enough to bring two worlds together. It should be defended at all costs!"

It was late afternoon when we reached Orihime's ISLAND. We found her with her father, standing on the bridge.

Orihime greeted us. "There you are! Were you successful with your mission?"

"Who are these intruders?" her father asked crossly. "We don't need any strangers around here. Especially not that wizard, Hikoboshi."

"Wow, he is really angry without the stone," Colette whispered.

Will approached him. "We are friends of your daughter, and we've come to give this back to you." Then he handed him the STONE. "My quartz!" the nymph's father exclaimed. "How did you get it? Why is there only half of it?"

Orihime's eyes widened, and I turned to her. "NAMAZU, the real owner of the stone, kept half for himself. He would like you to have the other half so that you can realize your dreams."

"Namazu? Dreams? What are you saying?" Orihime's father asked, **confused**.

"Orihime, the time has come to tell your father the *truth*," said a voice behind us. We turned to see Hikoboshi standing there!

"**YOU?**" the nymph's father exclaimed.

"I know that you don't want me to marry your daughter," the wizard said ***boldly***. "That is why I gave you the stone, to soften you and change your mind. But the stone was **NOT MINE** to take!"

Saying that, he took the quartz from the hands of Orihime's father and ***FLUNG*** it over the side of the bridge.

"What are you doing?" Orihime's father yelled.

"I was **WRONG**, and I ask everyone's forgiveness," Hikoboshi said humbly. "When you give me permission to marry your daughter it will be because you **RESPECT** me, and not because of the stone's power."

Taken by surprise, we all stood there in *silence*.

Then Hikoboshi continued. "My feelings

for you, Orihime, are STRONG and SINCERE. If it takes years for your father to understand that, I will wait!"

The nymph's eyes sparkled with happiness. She looked at her father, who turned to Hikoboshi.

"You have shown COURAGE," he said. "And most important, honesty. So I will give you a chance. But if you let me down, you have to forget my daughter forever."

Hikoboshi bowed respectfully to Orihime's father, and we could see that his eyes were filled with happy tears. Then he turned to Orihime and grasped her hands.

"I pledge my eternal love to you," he said.

"I have never heard you speak this way before," Orihime remarked. "You seem like someone else!"

"I feel different," Hikoboshi told her. "I

never should have **stolen** that stone from Namazu. Even if it had worked, our relationship would have been built on a **LIE**. And good things can only come from **truth**."

Then he turned to us. "I owe you all a great deal. You reminded me of what really matters, and you offered your help to me with no thought for yourselves. Thank you!"

"It was a **pleasure** to help you," I replied.

"Love, justice, and honesty are important to all of us," Colette added.

"And we love stories with **HAPPY ENDINGS**," Paulina concluded, smiling.

"We owe a lot to Namazu and his generosity," I pointed out. "Hikoboshi stole the thing that was most **PRECIOUS** to him, and when it was returned, he gave half of it up!"

Hikoboshi nodded. "It's true; he has set a very powerful **example** for all of us. This

evening I will return to ask his forgiveness, but first I will get the other HALF of the stone that I threw away and bring it back to him."

"The important thing is that everything ended well," Violet said.

The wizard grasped Orihime's hands once more. "Tomorrow I will begin to build a new home for us here, on the BRIDGE between our worlds!"

Then he said good-bye and walked away.

Orihime was beaming with *happiness*. She turned to us. "We would like to thank you for your help, and it's almost dinnertime. Won't you stay and eat with us?"

Pam's stomach GROWLED just hearing it, and we laughed.

"That's a definite yes!" I said.

Thank you for the dinner!

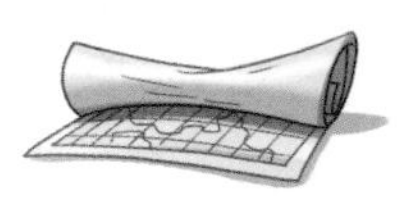

PAULINA'S MAP

"I slept so well!" Colette exclaimed as she woke up and stretched.

The night before, she had eyed the **FUTON** with suspicion. The traditional Japanese mattress was placed on the floor.

"I'm used to my Triple-Thick Extra Comfort

Beauty Sleep mattress," she had said. But she had been surprised at how **comfortable** the futon was.

We were all grateful for the hospitality of Orihime and her father. But it was time for us to return home. Paulina opened the **map** that she had drawn during the trip and laid it out on a table. She had **MARKED** all the places we had been to on the map.

I congratulated her. "This is great work!"

Will invited Orihime and her father to look at it. "Can you tell us if anything's missing, and help us complete it?"

"Of course," they replied.

We spent about an hour going over the map, perfecting the specifics of the **geography** of the Land of Minwa with their help.

"This will be very useful to the **INSTITUTE OF INCREDIBLE STORIES**," Will said, pleased.

That remark made our hosts curious, and they asked us about who we were and where we had come from. We answered without getting into details about the SEVEN ROSES UNIT. That had to remain a secret.

"You seem to be from a very strange place, but we are grateful that you came here to help us," Orihime said.

"And I will lend you a boat, so that you can more quickly reach the plain that you arrived on when you came here," her father added.

"Thank you so much," I said. "We will miss you."

"It's a shame that we can't stay for your wedding," Colette said sadly.

"You will be with us in spirit," Orihime promised, smiling sweetly.

And then it was time for us to go home.

We all said our good-byes.

"Come back and visit us!" Orihime called out, as we climbed into the boat.

Then we rowed away from our new friends.

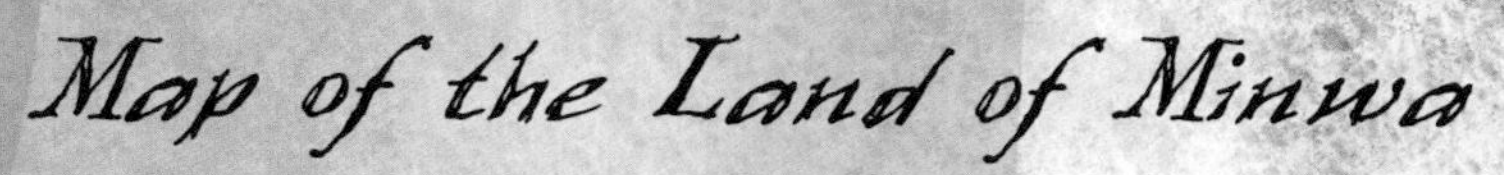

1. Sakura Forest
2. The Forest of the Dancing Pines
3. Devouring Sands Pond
4. The Bridge in the Fog
5. The Spirits' Cliff
6. The Blue Cave
7. The Swamp of Lost Dreams
8. The Crystal River
9. The Rounded Peak
10. The Bamboo Forest
11. The Musk Mountains
12. The Island of Sea Nymphs

11
12
9
10
7

A SURPRISING RETURN

We rowed the boat back to the end of the island where the glass elevator had landed. We docked the boat and then climbed out into a forest of pines.

"We should be CLOSE enough to the plains," Will said. "Let's form a circle and close our eyes."

We obeyed, and Will began to sing a song to call the elevator. When he finished, we opened our eyes.

NOTHING HAPPENED!

WE WERE ALL STILL THERE.

Then we heard muffled laughter coming from behind us.

We turned and saw an **old man** with a long beard that nearly touched the ground. He seemed very amused about something, and he came toward us, **chuckling** to himself.

"Why are you laughing?" Colette asked.

"You don't think you can **LEAVE** this land the same way you got here, do you?" he asked.

His voice had something **FAMILIAR** about it, but I couldn't figure out why.

The old man stopped a few steps away from us and looked at us, **scratching** his bald head.

"What do you mean?" I asked him.

"There is still something you must **LEARN** before you leave this world," the old man explained. "That is why you cannot leave."

"Do you mean that the **LAND OF MINWA** is hiding the elevator from us?" Colette asked, surprised.

"Something like that," the old man replied.

"And what is it that we need to learn?" Paulina asked.

"To find things with your **heart** instead of your eyes," he answered, looking down at Paulina's map. Then he gestured for us to follow him.

We walked through the trees out onto a vast, **snowy** plain. The gray winter sky seemed to blend into the horizon.

"Many poems have been written about the lotus flower through the centuries," the old man continued. "There is one, however, that explains how to grasp its **purest** essence."

"And how do you do that?" asked Violet.

"By losing yourself in its scent and beauty," he replied. "Sometimes, only by losing yourself is it possible to find your way."

Pam looked doubtful. "So we need **to get lost**?"

The sage nodded. "Exactly! That's how I found you: by getting lost. And that is how you solved the **mystery** of the lotus flowers. Thank you!"

Then his long beard began to shrink, his clothing sagged to the ground, and the face of one of our friends popped out from under the fabric: the **TANUKI**! "Hello, friends!" he greeted us.

"You **tricked** us

again!" Pam exclaimed.

We all burst out laughing.

"Thank you for all you have done for our land," the tanuki said, smiling.

"If there are other **problems**, you know how to find us," Will offered.

"But we still don't know how to get home," Colette pointed out.

"Can we trust the **advice** you've given us?" Nicky asked.

"Of course!" the tanuki replied. "From the first to the last word. And now if you'll excuse me, I must go to **SLEEP**. I should have been hibernating all this time, but with everything happening . . ."

Zzzzzz! Zzzzzz! Zzzzzz!

He had fallen asleep right on the spot! Will picked him up, took him back to the woods,

and put him carefully inside a hollow TREE to protect him from the snow.

"Sleep well, friend," Paulina whispered.

We all looked at him and felt a great sense of peace — the same peace that could now be felt all across the LAND OF MINWA.

We left the woods, and then, holding PAWS, began to walk across the plain with our EYES closed. We needed to "lose ourselves," just as the tanuki had advised.

And then, something happened.

GOOD-BYE!

We were walking with our eyes closed when suddenly I heard the faint SOUND of water lapping against the shore.

I opened my eyes. "Look!"

We were on the edge of a beautiful, clear lake. There was no more snow on the ground. The sun lit up the water, turning it into a shining mirror that reflected the majestic, snow-capped mountain across the lake.

"Mount Fuji!" Violet exclaimed.

"That's right," Will confirmed. "No other mountain in the world looks like it. So this means —"

"That we're in JAPAN!" Paulina concluded.

"What an enchanting landscape!" Colette exclaimed. "And it's in our world."

Mount Fuji!

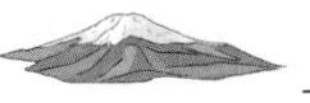

"Yes, and it's not any less fantastic than the Land of Minwa," said Violet.

"Do you know what this means?" Will asked.

"I know!" Pam cried. "We found the **SECRET PASSAGE** between the real Japan and the Land of Minwa."

"Will, do you think it works the same way on this side?" Nicky asked. "Can we reach the **LAND OF MINWA** by losing ourselves on the shore of this lake?"

"I think so," he replied. "In addition to the glass elevator, there is a secret passage to each fantasy world that can be found only by following your **imagination** . . . and I would say that we just found it!"

"I should mark this on the map," Paulina said.

"Good thinking, Paulina," Will said, and

she BEAMED at the compliment.

"This was an incredible experience," Violet remarked.

"And one that I trust you will never tell anyone," Will said. "Remember, all of the **missions** of the Seven Roses Unit are top secret!"

Colette grabbed the rose pendant she wore around her neck. It sparkled in the sun. "You can **TRUST** us!" she assured him.

"And now it's time to go," I interrupted. "Mouseford awaits!"

"Oh, that's right!" Pam cried. "We need to get back in time for the big holiday party. There's always such good food there. **Cheese** crackers, **cheese** dip, fried cheese, cheesecake . . ."

"Now you're making me hungry," Nicky said.

"Me, too," Colette agreed.

"We're not far from the city," Will said. "We can find TAXIS there to take us to the airport. I've got to head back to the I.I.S."

We left the lake and found our taxis easily. Will climbed into his and started to wave good-bye, but then Paulina suddenly remembered something.

"Wait, Will!" she called out. "The map!"

She ran toward the taxi, waving her map of the Land of Minwa. Then she ducked into the open window and handed it to Will.

"I totally forgot," Will said. "How scatterbrained of me."

Then he unfolded the paper, and his eyes widened in surprise. He hopped out of the cab and showed it to us, and we all gasped in shock.

The map was blank!

"Are you sure it's the right paper?" Violet asked.

"I'm sure," Paulina said. "I took very good care of it."

Will shook his head. "I think the map got **erased** somehow."

"But how?" Violet asked.

"Maybe some kind of magic?" Will guessed.

"THE PEN!" Paulina cried out. "The pen that the tanuki gave me. Remember? He insisted that I use it."

"So it was another one of his pranks," Paulina realized, disappointed.

Colette nodded. "We could read the map when we were in the LAND OF MINWA, but once we came to the real world, it disappeared."

"We must draw it again, before we forget," Will said. "And I can't do it alone. I will need all your HELP. How would you like to come back to the I.I.S. after your party?"

"Well, we don't have a CHOICE, do we?" I said, my eyes twinkling. "Of course we'll go back."

The Thea sisters cheered.

"HOORAY!" "HOORAY!" "HOORAY!" "HOORAY!" "HOORAY!"

"Then this isn't really good-bye," Will said with a grin. "It's just 'see you soon.'"

We gathered together for a big group hug, and then Will got back into his taxi. We waved as the driver took off.

"This is so exciting!" Paulina said. "Another trip to the I.I.S. Who knows what kind of adventure it will lead to?"

"We don't — which is what makes it so fun!" Colette responded.

I had to agree. We climbed into a taxi and headed to the airport. We had a huge celebration to go to at home, and then a trip to the Institute of Incredible Stories to look forward to.

IT DOESN'T GET ANY BETTER THAN THAT!

Don't miss any of my fabumouse special editions!

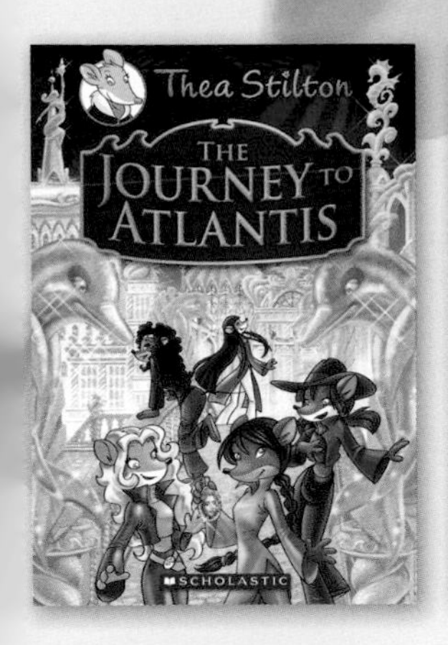

THE JOURNEY TO ATLANTIS

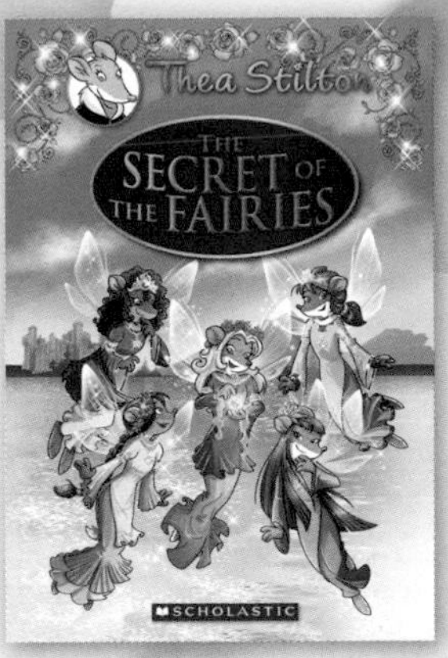

THE SECRET OF THE FAIRIES

THE SECRET OF THE SNOW

Check out these exciting Thea Sisters adventures!

Thea Stilton and the Dragon's Code

Thea Stilton and the Mountain of Fire

Thea Stilton and the Ghost of the Shipwreck

Thea Stilton and the Secret City

Thea Stilton and the Mystery in Paris

Thea Stilton and the Cherry Blossom Adventure

Thea Stilton and the Star Castaways

Thea Stilton: Big Trouble in the Big Apple

Thea Stilton and the Ice Treasure

Thea Stilton and the Secret of the Old Castl

Thea Stilton and the Blue Scarab Hunt

Thea Stilton and the Prince's Emerald

Thea Stilton and the Mystery on the Orient Express

Thea Stilton and the Dancing Shadows

Thea Stilton and the Legend of the Fire Flowe

Thea Stilton and the Spanish Dance Mission

Thea Stilton and the Journey to the Lion's Den

Thea Stilton and the Great Tulip Heist

Thea Stilton and the Chocolate Sabotage

Thea Stilton and the Missing Myth

Don't miss my adventures in the Kingdom of Fantasy!

THE KINGDOM OF FANTASY

THE QUEST FOR PARADISE:
THE RETURN TO THE KINGDOM OF FANTASY

THE AMAZING VOYAGE:
THE THIRD ADVENTURE IN THE KINGDOM OF FANTASY

THE DRAGON PROPHECY:
HE FOURTH ADVENTURE IN THE KINGDOM OF FANTASY

THE VOLCANO OF FIRE:
THE FIFTH ADVENTURE IN THE KINGDOM OF FANTASY

THE SEARCH FOR TREASURE:
THE SIXTH ADVENTURE IN THE KINGDOM OF FANTASY

Be sure to read these stories, too!

#1 Lost Treasure of the Emerald Eye

#2 The Curse of the Cheese Pyramid

#3 Cat and Mouse in a Haunted House

#4 I'm Too Fond of My Fur!

#5 Four Mice Deep in the Jungle

#6 Paws Off, Cheddarface!

#7 Red Pizzas for a Blue Count

#8 Attack of the Bandit Cats

#9 A Fabumouse Vacation for Geronimo

#10 All Because of a Cup of Coffee

#11 It's Halloween, You 'Fraidy Mouse!

#12 Merry Christmas, Geronimo!

#13 The Phantom of the Subway

#14 The Temple of the Ruby of Fire

#15 The Mona Mousa Code

#16 A Cheese-Colored Camper

#17 Watch Your Whiskers, Stilton!

#18 Shipwreck on the Pirate Islands

#19 My Name Is Stilton, Geronimo Stilton

#20 Surf's Up, Geronimo!

#21 The Wild, Wild West

#22 The Secret of Cacklefur Castle

A Christmas Tale

#23 Valentine's Day Disaster

#24 Field Trip to Niagara Falls

#25 The Search for Sunken Treasure

#26 The Mummy with No Name

#27 The Christmas Toy Factory

#28 Wedding Crasher

#29 Down and Out Down Under

#30 The Mouse Island Marathon

#31 The Mysterious Cheese Thief

Christmas Catastrophe

#32 Valley of the Giant Skeletons

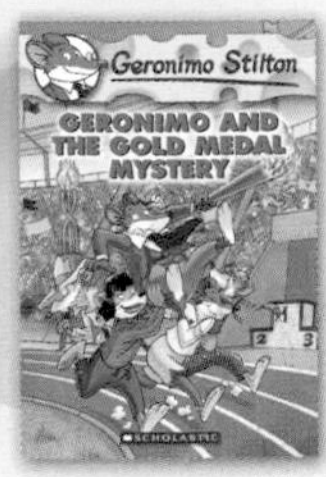

#33 Geronimo and the Gold Medal Mystery

#34 Geronimo Stilton, Secret Agent

#35 A Very Merry Christmas

#36 Geronimo's Valentine

#37 The Race Across America

#38 A Fabumouse School Adventure

#39 Singing Sensation

#40 The Karate Mouse

#41 Mighty Mount Kilimanjaro

#42 The Peculiar Pumpkin Thief

#43 I'm Not a Supermouse!

#44 The Giant Diamond Robbery

#45 Save the White Whale!

#46 The Haunted Castle

#47 Run for the Hills, Geronimo!

#48 The Mystery in Venice

#49 The Way of the Samurai

#50 This Hotel Is Haunted!

#51 The Enormouse Pearl Heist

#52 Mouse in Space!

#53 Rumble in the Jungle

#54 Get into Gear, Stilton!

#55 The Golden Statue Plot

#56 Flight of the Red Bandit

The Hunt for the Golden Book

#57 The Stinky Cheese Vacation

#58 The Super Chef Contest

#59 Welcome to Moldy Manor

Don't miss my journey through time!